Danger on the Seine

As they turned up the street leading to Mimi's building, something caught Nancy's eye. "Wait a minute," she said to George. "Look. Look out there. Do you see that . . . there, on the river?"

George followed Nancy's gaze and squinted her eyes. Although it was night, the city was bathed in light from streetlamps, candlelit outdoor cafés, and occasional boats bobbing along the Seine.

"There's something out there," George said. "Do you mean that white thing floating on the river?" Just as she spoke, a barge loaded with tourists chugged by, and the clump of white disappeared under the wake. In a few minutes, it bobbed back up, continuing its wavy journey.

"The person who leaped out of Bess's room had something white in his or her left hand," Nancy reminded George.

"Yeah, but that could be anything floating out there," George said. "A piece of paper, a food carton, a loaf of bread . . ."

"A marionette," Nancy added.

Nancy Drew
Mystery Stories

Available from Simon & Schuster

NANCY DREW® 170

NO STRINGS ATTACHED

CAROLYN KEENE

Aladdin Paperbacks
New York   London   Toronto   Sydney   Singapore

First Aladdin Paperbacks edition January 2003

Copyright © 2003 by Simon & Schuster, Inc.

ALADDIN PAPERBACKS
An imprint of Simon & Schuster
Children's Publishing Division
1230 Avenue of the Americas
New York, NY 10020

Printed in the United States of America

10 9 8 7 6 5 4 3

NANCY DREW, NANCY DREW MYSTERY STORIES, and colophon are registered trademarks of Simon & Schuster, Inc.

Library of Congress Control Number 2002109948

ISBN 0-689-85559-1

Contents

1

The Stage Is Set

The Monday morning sun bounced off the Seine and right into Nancy Drew's clear blue eyes. "This is it," she said, stopping at a pretty brick building. She read one of the posters that hung under a small marquee and translated it from French to English. "Juliette's Marionettes Presents Original Parisian Folktales, Adapted by Mimi Loiseau. Also Featuring Selected Scenes from the Classics of Literature."

Next to the theater door was another door labeled MUSÉE DES MARIONETTES. "Looks like she has a museum, too," Bess Marvin said. Bess was Nancy's age, seventeen, and she had the same blue eyes. But her hair was curlier and blonder than Nancy's reddish gold waves. She peeked in the window. "And a shop. Great! There goes my vacation budget."

"Budget!" George Fayne said with a whoop of laughter. "That'll be the day—you setting a budget for a vacation in Paris." George was Bess's cousin, but you could never tell by looking at her. Also seventeen, George was tall, with brown eyes and a cap of chestnut hair. She had the lean, muscular body of an accomplished athlete.

"Hey, a little respect, please," Bess said. "You wouldn't even be here if it weren't for me and my frequent-flyer miles. A round-trip ticket to Paris for two hundred dollars is an awesome deal."

"Absolutely," Nancy said. She was used to the bickering between her two best friends. "Let's check out the apartment my dad scored for us."

Both doors were locked, so Nancy rang the museum bell. A pretty brunette dressed in jeans and a black turtleneck answered the door. Tall and slim, she had huge dark eyes and a stylish haircut. Nancy figured the woman was in her early thirties.

"You must be Nancy," she said. "I'm Mimi Loiseau. I've been expecting you." She ushered them in, and Nancy introduced her friends.

"We'll have plenty of time for a tour of the place later," Mimi said. "Right now, I'm sure you'd like to get settled." She led them upstairs. "The first floor is the museum, shop, and theater," she told them as they climbed the stairs. "I live in the second-floor apartment." She opened a glass double door

2

on the top floor. "And this is yours."

The apartment had a living room, tiny kitchen, two bedrooms, and a large bath. A door led to a small balcony. "I'm going to lunch at my favorite café," Mimi said. "Would you like to join me?" The girls nodded; they hadn't eaten since the flight. Nancy was glad that Mimi spoke such good English. She and the girls had meant to brush up on their French during the flight, but slept most of the way!

They all walked two short blocks to Chèz Sylvie. The streets were narrow and lined with very old, very beautiful houses. Nancy felt as if she were in another world. Sprinkled among the houses were quaint specialty stores, pâtisseries, and art galleries.

Chèz Sylvie was a charming café with an outdoor court on the bank of the Seine. "You'll love this place," Mimi said. "They make the best ice cream—from scratch!"

Nancy and her friends ordered sandwiches, sodas, and ice cream for dessert. Mimi ordered soup, tea, and ice cream. When their drinks arrived, Mimi had a toast for the girls: "Welcome to Île Saint-Louis, an island in the middle of Paris!"

The four spent the next hour eating and sharing stories of previous experiences in Paris. They were sitting just a few yards from a wide bridge—the Pont Saint-Louis—which stretched across the Seine. On the opposite bank, a sprawling building hugged the edge of the river. Behind it rose a thin spire. "That's Notre-Dame," Mimi said, nodding toward the spire. "This bridge leads to a second tiny island, Île de la Cité. Notre-Dame sits on that island."

"I've been to Paris twice, but somehow I never realized there were two islands in the middle of the Seine," Bess said.

"The Parisii tribe settled on the Île de la Cité in 553 B.C.," Mimi told them. "That island has always been called the heart of Paris. Île Saint-Louis is mostly residential. The apartments and houses have been passed down for generations. Some residents think of it almost like a tiny country all its own. When they cross the bridges that connect it with the rest of the city, they say they are 'going to Paris.' It's a pretty special place."

"This ice cream is way more than special," Bess said. "It's awesome!" She took a spoonful of the strawberry-peach ice cream and swirled it around in her mouth.

"I saw from one of the posters outside your building that you're doing a show tonight," Nancy said, bringing Mimi's attention back to the table.

"Yes, and it might be my last one, aside from a fair this weekend," Mimi said. Tears welled up in her eyes.

"Is it the end of your season or something?" George asked.

4

"More like the end of my business," Mimi responded softly. She sat back in her chair and picked at her ice cream with a cookie.

Mimi was quiet for a minute, then continued, her voice stronger. "Well, you might as well know, since you'll be staying here. I don't want you to worry about your apartment. No matter what happens to my other enterprises, your place in the house will still be secure for as long as you stay in Paris."

She pushed her ice cream around with the cookie. "I don't know how much your father told you about my business, Nancy, but . . ." She paused.

"He said your father was a fourth-generation puppetmaker, and that you inherited the family marionette museum and theater," Nancy replied.

"Which I have pretty much destroyed, it seems," Mimi said. "I have tried to make it work, but I'm afraid I made some bad business choices along the way. When my business first began to fail, I opened the shop. It broke my heart to sell some of the family treasures, but I had no choice if the museum and theater were going to survive. Now, even selling the puppets is not helping. I must do the show tonight because some people have already bought tickets. Besides, I need the rehearsal before the weekend—especially since I no longer have Quentin."

"Who's he?" George asked. "One of the puppets you had to sell?"

"Oh, my, no," Mimi said, her eyes opening even larger. For the first time since they'd sat down, she smiled. "Quentin DuBos is—*was*—my best puppeteer. I had to let the others go, but I didn't want to lose him. He was so good, and the only help I had left. Then I reached a point a couple of weeks ago when I could no longer afford even Quentin full time. I asked him if he would consider contract work—just being paid by the show. He was very insulted and stormed off. He hasn't been back since."

"What exactly is the show this weekend?" Nancy asked.

"It's a big one," Mimi said, finally taking a bite of ice cream. "It's a country fair, actually, out of town, at Château de Berc. I'm doing a marionette version of *The Hunchback of Notre-Dame*. I'm including one of the scenes from it in the show tonight, as well as some old Parisian legends that I've written into skits. I hope we have a full house."

Nancy felt a pull to help the young woman. "We were actually thinking of coming to the show," Nancy said. "We haven't done much work with marionettes, but is there anything we could do to help you backstage beforehand? Maybe set up and change scenery—stuff like that?"

"Oh, yes," Bess said. "I'd love to do that!" George nodded her agreement.

"There's lots you could do," Mimi said, "but I

really can't let you. I couldn't pay anything."

"I know," Nancy said. "But it would be fun—and you obviously could use the help."

Mimi looked at Nancy for a moment. "I've done these shows so many times, I can practically do them in my sleep," she said. "But it *would* help so much to have some extra hands."

She sat forward in her chair and smiled at the girls. "I'll tell you what," she said. "Let's try it for tonight. If it works, and if you want to, you can come to the country fair with me this weekend. It's a huge charity event. It costs a lot to get in, and even those who can afford it need a special invitation. But if you go as my troupe, you'll get in for free. We'll have plenty of free time to wander around and see everything too. There's lots of fun scheduled: music, dancing, food, sports competitions, a fashion show, and tons more."

"Sounds pretty cool," Nancy said. "Let's give it a trial run tonight and see how it works."

"Great!" Mimi said, standing. "Meet me back at the theater at six o'clock, and I'll walk you through everything."

Nancy and her friends watched Mimi walk away from the tables in the outdoor café and disappear down a narrow alley.

"Well, what do you think?" Nancy asked, sipping her soda.

"The fair sounds wonderful," Bess said. "It'd be a great chance to spend a weekend at a real French château. And it sounds like there's plenty of fun things to do while we're there."

"She did say we wouldn't have to work that much," George added. "I wonder if they'll have any archery competitions. That'd be cool."

"Okay, we'll see how tonight goes," Nancy agreed. "And then we'll decide."

Nancy, Bess, and George left Chèz Sylvie and walked across the Pont Saint-Louis to Île de la Cité. Once on the island, they walked along a street lined with old trees and little shops until they came to the back of Notre-Dame.

Nancy led them through the gardens and around to the large courtyard in the front. Tight bands of tourists followed their guides from the buses into the majestic Gothic building. Nancy and her friends slipped past the crowds and entered Notre-Dame.

"Wow," Nancy said, as soon as she got inside. It was dark and sort of gloomy. "I can't get over how old this place feels," she added. They passed the famous rose window, with its thousands of hand-cut, brightly colored images. Gilded carvings shone from the stone walls, and the high arched ceiling seemed to shelter them with its graceful Gothic arches.

Nancy headed straight for the stairway. Three hundred and eighty-seven steps later, she was eye-to-eye with a fanged stone creature perched on the corner of the roof. He was sitting up, his hands resting on his knee.

"Now that's one sassy gargoyle," Bess said. "He looks like he owns the city."

"That's not a gargoyle," George said. "I learned that on my last visit. Gargoyles are the rainspout ones that hang way over the side. This guy's a chimera. He's just there to look pretty."

"Pretty, hmmmm?" Bess muttered. "Oh, look at that," she said, walking over to see the bell called Emmanuel. "I read that this weighs thirteen tons. Ringing that baby would be one tough job."

"Technology has arrived in Notre-Dame," Nancy said. "It's rung electronically now." After spending a little more time drinking in the incredible view, they started back down the stairway.

"I never get tired of seeing the panorama from the top of this building," George said.

"You can take a tour of nothing but rooftop views," Nancy said. "You go to the top of the Montparnasse Tower, the Sacré Coeur dome, the Arc de Triomphe, and the Eiffel Tower."

"Cool," George said. "Let's do it!"

"Great," Bess said. "I'll make reservations."

Nancy and her friends strolled back across the bridge to Île Saint-Louis and made their way to the puppet theater. Mimi had figured out some interesting things they could do to help with the show, without having to learn a lot.

"I'm going to do a scene with just Quasimodo and play a tape of narration," she said. "That way, we'll need only one puppeteer: me. You three can make crowd noises when I cue you and help with the sets and lighting. Nancy, you can ring Emmanuel. We're also going to do a couple of Parisian legend skits, but you should be able to handle them just fine. I can't tell you how much I appreciate this help."

The rehearsals went well, and before the show they took a break to change clothes. Mimi gave them black slim pants and black high-necked, long-sleeved knit shirts. "These are the costumes worn by my family for generations," she explained.

Mimi was gratified to see the small theater fill up. The air was filled with the sounds of laughing children and chattering adults.

During a break while they were waiting to change a set for one of the legend skits, George and Nancy whispered in one of the wings. "It's going pretty well, don't you think?" George said quietly.

Nancy barely heard her over the folk music tape. "Mmm-hmm," Nancy agreed. "The audience seems to love it—especially the kids."

"You know, this place *could* use a little upgrading," George said, looking around. "I didn't notice it before, but have you caught that smell? It's pretty stinky."

Nancy took a few tentative sniffs, then a deeper one. As the smell grew stronger, she tensed. "It's coming from back near that door," she said, turning toward the door. "George, look!"

Nancy pointed to the bottom of the door at the back of the wing. A smudgy gray plume of smoke twirled and twisted toward them.

2

Mimi's Mystery

"Nancy, it's a fire!" George said, whispering loudly. She raced toward the door.

"Don't open it," Nancy warned. "It'll make the smoke worse." She raced up the steps to the platform where Mimi and Bess stood controlling the marionettes on the stage below. Once Nancy told Mimi what was happening, she dropped her marionette and raced to the phone.

While Mimi called the fire station, Bess announced to the audience that there was an emergency, the show was over, and that they must leave. She and Mimi helped everyone get out safely.

George aimed an antiquated fire extinguisher at the bottom of the door. Nancy pulled the hose in from the courtyard garden and soaked the door with water.

"It's my storage room," Mimi said. "There's another door to the alley in back. I've got to get in there." She raced out through the courtyard. Nancy chased after her, determined to keep her out of the burning room. By the time they reached the alley, the firemen had arrived. It didn't take long for them to finish extinguishing the flames.

"Thanks to your quick work, the fire is over," the chief announced in halting English to Nancy and the others. "But we recommend that you do not try to fight fires yourself. That is what we are for."

"This little room was a real fire trap," one of the other firemen said, shaking his head. "He held up a torn, cloth-covered cord. "You need to replace the electrical wiring in this building. You're very lucky that the fire didn't spread."

He took a few scraps of cloth from the burned costumes and an ash-filled metal wastebasket from the storage room and joined the rest of his crew as they left the theater.

Bess put her arm around Mimi's shoulders to comfort her.

"I can't believe it," Mimi said, shaking her head. She reached down to pick up a charred piece of wood. Sprigs of black and gray poked out here and there from the long round column. "This is a spare leg for Red Riding Hood's wolf," she said, pulling out one of the gray strands and holding it up. "My

13

great-grandfather used real wolf hair."

"Wow, you really meant it when you said some of this stuff couldn't be replaced," George said, sensing the hurt in Mimi's voice.

"Come on," Nancy said. "Let's air the room out for a while. Then we'll help you clean up." She and Mimi set up a couple of fans to blow the thick smoky air out into the alley. A few people in the crowd of onlookers spoke to Mimi, extending their regrets and offering encouragement. Gradually they all shuffled away.

Nancy, Bess, George, and Mimi started across the stage toward the back stairway that led to Mimi's apartment. Shouts from behind stopped them.

"Mimi! Mimi, are you all right?" A tall attractive man dressed in jeans and a long-sleeved polo shirt ran toward them. Nancy guessed he was around Mimi's age.

"William! I was just going to call you." Mimi kissed each of his cheeks twice, one after the other. She introduced the man as William Smythe, her friend and attorney. William took her arm and steered her toward the stairway. Nancy and the others followed.

"I was down at the café when I heard," William said. "I am so sorry, my dear. What happened?"

"Probably bad wiring," Mimi said. "The fireman said I have to replace it all. Just one more thing I can't afford to do."

"I've told you what to do about this place,"

William said, steering Mimi into her kitchen. "When are you going to start listening?"

Mimi filled the tea kettle and put it on the stove. Then she filled a plate with chunks of cheese and sliced meat. "William's partner, Christophe Binet, wants to buy my business," she said, handing Nancy a basket of crusty French bread. "William thinks it's a good idea."

"It *is* a good idea," William said. "This whole enterprise is too much for you to handle."

"Perhaps," Mimi responded. "But it doesn't have to be. If I can just find—"

William put his hand up. "Please," he urged, "stop right there. I don't want to hear any more about the great family treasure. I'm convinced it's just a myth, perpetrated by that bizarre great-grandmother of yours. She was a storyteller, that's all."

"Treasure?" Nancy repeated. "Sounds interesting."

Mimi frowned at Nancy and shook her head lightly. Nancy realized that Mimi wanted her to change the subject, so she did. "Does Christophe have any experience running a theater or museum?" Nancy asked.

"No, he doesn't," Mimi responded quickly. "Please, everyone, let's enjoy our food and forget my worries for the moment."

After they finished their meal, they all went back to the storage room to begin the cleanup. Nancy helped Mimi begin to assess some of the damage and sort through the items that could be saved. Bess and George swept up shards of glass and scraps of charred wood.

After William swabbed the puddles of water that were left by the firemen, he rehung the door that led from the back of the storage room to the alley. Then Mimi urged him to go on home. "We're not going to do much more now," she told him. "I'm so tired." Nancy could tell that her new friend was too distressed to go through any more of the ruins that night.

William smiled at Mimi and nodded. "We'll get a fresh start in the morning," he said. "Meanwhile, let me call Christophe and set up a meeting for you. At least hear what he has to say, okay?"

"All right, all right," Mimi said with a sigh. "But I'm not promising anything."

William left, and Nancy helped Mimi pull a large standing screen over the opening from the stage to the storage room. Then they all closed up the theater and went back upstairs.

"Please don't go to your apartment yet," Mimi said. "We never had our dessert." She seemed to be on the verge of tears.

Nancy could tell that Mimi didn't want to be alone yet, so she, Bess, and George sat down at the tiny breakfast table. Over slices of lemon nut cake, Nancy gently asked Mimi about her plans.

"My plans for tomorrow, or for my life?" Mimi asked back.

"Well, let's start with tomorrow," Nancy answered. "You don't seem to be looking forward to the meeting with Christophe."

"I'm not," Mimi said. "William is a good friend, but he has been pressuring me to sell my business for some time. He says that Christophe wants to continue the museum and theater and hire me to run them. But I'm not sure that Christophe's interest is really in preserving my family's heritage. What if he's just interested in the valuable real estate?"

"Don't you trust William and Christophe?" George asked.

"It's not exactly that I don't trust them," Mimi answered. "I think William really wants the best for me, and sometimes I'm almost tempted to sell my business and move away from expensive Paris to a little village in the country. But I don't think William understands what these puppets mean to me. If this theater is closed, it will be the end of my family's generations of puppetry on the Île Saint-Louis. That would break my heart."

Then Nancy asked the question she had been dying to ask since supper. "What's this family treasure you mentioned earlier?"

"My great-grandmother Juliette had always hinted at something unique and very valuable in our family;

17

an inherited prize that would one day be mine. If I could only figure out what or where this wonderful inheritance is, it might save my business."

"And you don't have any idea at all about what it is?" Bess asked.

"No," Mimi answered. "I've been trying to solve this mystery nearly all my life. So had my father. But he died three years ago, without figuring it out. My mother died very young, so I could never talk to her about it."

Nancy felt a pang of recognition and kinship. Nancy's mother had died when Nancy was three, and her father had worked extra hard to keep Nancy's life full and happy. Still, she missed her mother, and this gave her a special bond with Mimi. "Maybe we can help," she offered.

"William doesn't seem to believe there even is a treasure, does he?" observed Bess.

"I've told him a lot about Juliette," Mimi explained. "He knows that she loved riddles and puzzles. I think he figures the inheritance story was all a game to her—or maybe that whatever the treasure is, it's long gone by now. I don't know, maybe he's right. Perhaps it was just a tale concocted by Juliette."

"If there's a treasure, Nancy will find it," Bess pointed out. "She is a very well-known detective back home. She's solved many tough cases. I'm sure she can crack this one."

"Really?" For the first time since the fire, Mimi's eyes sparkled with something besides tears. "Nancy, do you really think you could help me?"

"I can try," Nancy said. "Tell me about your other relatives. Do any of them have any clues about where this inheritance might be?"

"There are very few people left in my family," Mimi answered. "Just a couple of cousins. I don't know them very well. Juliette had always lived with my father's family, and he didn't think anyone else knew her story."

"Was the treasure supposed to be something that must be found or discovered?" Nancy asked. She felt a flutter of excitement. "Or was it supposed to be something that would just be presented at a specific time, like an inheritance?"

"That's a good question," Mimi said. "Juliette died before she told us exactly what she meant. Come into the salon. I want to show you something."

Mimi led Nancy and her friends into the living room and over to a wood bureau. It had five drawers, each one painted with beautiful pictures of animals and birds. When Mimi pulled out the third drawer, the front of the drawer dropped down to reveal a desk lined with cubbyholes and smaller drawers. Each compartment was stuffed with letters, newspaper clippings, postcards, and small leather-bound books.

Mimi opened the other four drawers to reveal

more papers, books, and cards. "Here it all is," she said. "Juliette's bureau, and all her things. I've been through everything many times, and have not yet found a specific reference to treasure or inheritance or legacy of any kind. Help yourself—feel free to go through all of this."

The chirpy trill of Mimi's phone called her away. When she left to answer it, Nancy began poking through the drawers. Someone had taken a stab at organizing the contents. Posters, flyers, and programs from various puppet shows filled one drawer and half of another. Letters to and from Juliette brimmed over from the fourth drawer into the fifth.

"Whoa, there's a lot of junk here," George said.

"There sure is," Nancy said. "Some of this stuff can be checked pretty fast."

"It still looks like it's going to take a while to get through all of this," George said. "And this time, I'm here to play some tennis. I haven't seen Veronique since she came to River Heights for that invitational tournament last year. She's organized some doubles matches for us while I'm here."

"I really want to help Mimi," Bess added. "I feel sorry for her, and this does sound like a cool mystery. But I'm not leaving Paris without getting in some shopping and sight-seeing."

"Agreed," Nancy said.

Bess pulled a packet of letters from one of the

desk compartments and untied the pale blue ribbon that held them together. "My French isn't outstanding," she said, "but I can probably figure some of this out."

George rifled through the top drawer of the bureau. "You know, Bess," she said, "some day we're going to learn that going on vacation with Nancy isn't always your average—"

"Oh, this is terrible!" Mimi cried, rejoining them in the salon. Her face was very pale. "It's terrible!"

"What happened?" Nancy asked.

"That was the fire examiner!" Mimi exclaimed. "It was . . . he said . . . they think the fire was *arson*!"

3

Stage Fright

"Arson?" Bess repeated.

"Who would do such a thing?" Mimi said. "Why?"

"Has anything like this ever happened before?" Nancy asked. "Has anyone ever threatened you, or tried to harm you or your business?"

"No," Mimi said slowly. "Well . . . I have noticed a few things missing lately," she added, looking off into the distance. "But I . . . I'm sure I just mislaid them."

She slowly paced between the bureau and the sofa. "The fire examiner told me not to clean up the mess until they could check it all. I told him we'd already started. He said to stop and to save the trash we'd already collected. He'll have a team over here first thing in the morning."

"Why don't you try to get some sleep," Nancy said.

"It's late, and it's been a really rough day. We'll talk about all this again in the morning, okay?"

"All right," Mimi said. She flashed a weak smile. "Thank you all for your help. Look through anything you want from the bureau." She padded slowly off toward her bedroom.

Nancy leafed through a couple of the leather-bound books in the desk and selected one to examine more carefully. George grabbed a large envelope full of programs and articles about the theater and its productions. Bess picked up the packet of letters she had untied. With these things, the three started toward the double doors at the end of Mimi's living room and headed up the stairway which led to their apartment.

"Mmmm, wait a minute," Nancy said. "I left my notebook in the theater. You two go ahead. I'll be right up."

Nancy walked back through Mimi's kitchen to the back staircase leading to the museum and theater. *I just want one good look around before the fire crew gets here tomorrow,* she told herself as she stepped on the wood floor of the stage and switched on the work light.

The girls' footsteps and fingerprints had already contaminated the area from the earlier cleanup, so she knew she shouln't even worry about that. But she didn't want to move anything clse that might be lying around. So very carefully—without disturbing any possible evidence—Nancy checked over the fire-damaged storage room to see if she could find any clues. Only three items didn't seem to fit: a partially burned small black card, a torn paycheck stub from a restaurant named Pascal's, and a box of matches with the picture of a three-cornered hat on it.

Without touching these things, Nancy took out her pad and jotted down notes describing the items and where they were located. Then she sketched the black card and the three-cornered hat on the matchbox.

When she got back up to the apartment, Bess and George were already in their beds, surrounded by the items they had taken from Juliette's bureau. Nancy told them what she'd seen in the storage room and showed them the sketch of the three-cornered hat.

"The pay stub wasn't even scorched," Nancy pointed out to her friends. "Neither was the matchbox. They were lying on the floor in the path of the fire, so they couldn't have been there before it started—or they'd at least be charred."

"What are you saying?" George asked.

"That either one could have been dropped by the person who started the fire," Nancy concluded.

"What's this card thing?" Bess asked, looking at the sketch of the black rectangle.

"I recognize that. It's called a *Paris Visite* card," Nancy said. "We'll get some tomorrow. It's a discount pass for public transportation. You buy one of these ahead of time. Then you get unlimited travel for five days on the bus, the train that goes around the city, and the Métro—the Paris subway."

"Did the pay stub have any other information besides the name Pascal's?" George asked.

"It was torn," Nancy reported, "and the employee's name was ripped off. I'm going over to Pascal's tomorrow to look around."

Bess and George snuggled down under their covers and started looking through the letters and clippings from Juliette's bureau. Nancy put on her pajamas and padded over to her old iron bed. She fell asleep reading Juliette's journal.

Tuesday morning, over croissants, jam, milk, and tea, Nancy, Bess, and George talked about their late-night reading. None of them had found any reference to the family legacy.

"Good morning." Mimi rapped softly on the door of their apartment, then poked her head through. "You *are* up. I thought I heard activity up here. I brought you some maps and brochures; a lot's happening in Paris this week." Nancy thought that the night's sleep had been good for Mimi. She seemed calmer, and was smiling.

"Great!" Bess said, eagerly taking the stack of papers from Mimi.

"So, do you have anything planned?" Mimi asked, joining them at the table beneath the window. From their third-floor apartment, they could see barges and houseboats chugging along the Seine. "It's a beautiful day."

Nancy told Mimi what she had discovered in the storage room the night before, and what it could mean.

"No one has access to that storage room but me," Mimi said. She seemed rattled by Nancy's find. "Most people don't even know it's there."

"But there *is* the door from the alley," Nancy pointed out. "So anyone could break in."

"I guess you're right," Mimi said. The cheery tone had left her voice, and the worried look returned to her eyes.

"Are any of the items I saw yours, by any chance?" Nancy asked.

Mimi looked at the list in Nancy's notebook. "No . . . no, they aren't," she said quietly. "I don't own a *Visite* card. And I've never been to Pascal's," she added, scanning the paycheck stub. "It's a bistro across the river, on the Left Bank. It's on Boulevard Saint-Germain. To get there, you'd have to go to Île de la Cité. Then walk over the Petit Pont to the Left Bank."

"How about the matchbox Nancy saw?" George asked.

"The three-cornered hat is the logo of a private club, Le Tricorne," Mimi told them. "I'm not a member, but William is. Christophe probably is too. William could have dropped it any time he was here, I suppose. Even last night, while we cleaned up."

"When is the fire examiner coming?" Nancy asked.

"He said sometime after nine o'clock," Mimi answered, checking her watch. "That's a half-hour from now. I'd better get down there and open up the place. I want to see the items you found too."

"I'm coming with you," Nancy said. "I'd like one last look around."

George and Bess wanted to go too, so Mimi led all three of them down the back stairway, past the second floor and her apartment, and into the main floor. She left the museum closed and locked, and they walked into the lobby of the theater. Mimi unlocked the door from the inside, so the fire examiner could come in.

Nancy took the lead, guiding the others down the aisle toward the stage, which was masked with its heavy purple velvet curtain. "Remember, everyone," she said, "look, but don't touch. We may have smeared our fingerprints all over everything else, but we don't want to contaminate the *Visite* card, the matchbox, or the paycheck stub. They could be—"

Suddenly Nancy stopped and held her hands out to stop the others. She signaled for quiet and strained her ears toward the stage.

At first she heard nothing. Then a faint scratching noise filtered through the heavy curtain. In her mind, Nancy pictured a mouse scampering across the boards of the stage floor.

It was quiet for a few moments. Then she heard a clattering clunk, as if something with several parts had fallen to the floor. Nancy gestured for the others to be still. Bess clamped her hand across her mouth, and her eyes grew large.

Nancy tiptoed up the short wooden stairway to the wing area at one side of the stage. The light was very dim, but she could see that the screen had been pulled away from the opening to the storage room. A dark form crouched on the floor. Next to the person lay a crumpled marionette.

Nancy slid along the wall until she felt the light switch. She held her breath and flicked the switch.

The form jumped up—a man. The shock on his face turned to menace when he saw Nancy. Without a word, he started toward her.

4

Busted at the Bistro

The man crept slowly toward Nancy. Behind her, she heard her friends pounding up the stairway and onto the stage. "Who are you?" Nancy said firmly, holding her ground. "Who are you?" she repeated when he didn't answer. "What are you doing here? This is a crime scene. Examiners are on their way to gather evidence."

The man stopped coming toward her, but he kept his menacing glare. He started to speak but stopped when the others ran up.

"Claude!" Mimi cried. Then she and the man began a lively conversation in French. They spoke at a furious pace, but Nancy could understand some of it. There was no mistaking the tone of the conversation. Both speakers were angry.

"This is my father's cousin, Claude Loiseau," Mimi said finally. "He was just leaving."

The man glared at Mimi with the same menace that he had shown toward Nancy. He turned and stomped off the stage to the exit door.

When the door closed behind him, Mimi crumpled onto an old iron bench. Her face was flushed, and her hands trembled. Nancy sat beside her.

"I'm sorry," Mimi said. "He made me so angry."

"I heard you talking about the fire," Nancy said. "Do you think he had something to do with it?"

"I'm afraid so," Mimi said nodding her head. "I didn't want to say anything to you all about it, because it's so embarrassing. A part of my family's history I would rather forget . . ."

"You don't have to tell us anything you don't want to," Nancy said gently.

"No, no, it's okay," Mimi said. "You have offered to help me, and I am so grateful for that. No one believes that there really is a treasure, so you're my last hope. And I know you need to know as much as possible." She stood up and began to pace.

"Claude has bugged me off and on ever since my father died," Mimi said. "He comes over or calls every few months."

"What does he want?" George asked.

"He's always trying to get me to turn over the museum and theater to him," Mimi said. "He doesn't have the money to buy it, so I'd still own it. But he'd run it for me. He says he can turn it around and really make it successful." She stopped pacing and looked at Nancy. "But I just don't trust him," she added. "I remember my parents talking about Claude. They used to call him 'the family problem,' because he'd occasionally get into trouble with the law."

"Does he know about the treasure?" Nancy asked.

"My father asked him once, but Claude said he didn't know anything about it. I don't think Father believed him." Mimi plunked back down on the bench. "I'd like to think Claude has changed, but I'm afraid to risk going into business with him."

"What did he say he was doing back here?" Nancy asked.

"Same old thing. He said he came to talk to me about running the theater," Mimi said. "But you saw him. He was definitely snooping around back here."

"Have you told anyone else about Claude?" Nancy asked. "William, maybe? As your attorney, he might say something to Claude about staying away from you. Or you might even consider telling the police, if he's actually been threatening you."

"It hasn't really gone that far until now," Mimi said. "I never had anything really substantial to tell anyone—just a bad feeling. But now, with the fire—"

"Excuse me," a strange voice called out. "Is there anyone up there? I'm looking for Mimi Loiseau."

31

Mimi pulled back the curtain, and Nancy saw the fire examiner and a policeman standing in the audience aisle. Mimi showed them the stairway and invited them up. While they waited, Nancy quickly scanned the storage room. The Le Tricorne matchbox and the pay stub were exactly as she had left them. Something was missing, though.

"Mimi, the *Visite* card is gone," Nancy said. "And it was on the floor in the same general area where Claude was kneeling when I first saw him."

"He took it!" Mimi said, her voice hushed.

"It looks like it," Nancy said. *Was that why he was here?* she wondered. *Was it his card, and he came back today to retrieve it—along with the incriminating fingerprints that might be on it?*

"I didn't see him actually pick it up," Nancy continued aloud, "or even see him put something in his pocket when I surprised him. But if you want to tell the investigators about Claude, I'll stay and tell them what I did see."

"Yes, please do," Mimi said, then went to greet the men.

After Mimi talked briefly with them, Nancy gave her statement. Mimi told the policeman briefly about Claude. Nancy then pointed out the marionette on the floor, which had not been there the night before. She explained that the falling doll might have been the source of the clattering noise they had heard. Finally, she showed them where the *Visite* card had been.

The examiner and the policeman both took notes. Then they began the tedious job of exploring the storage room for other clues.

"We're going to leave," Nancy said. "I want to check out Pascal's and Le Tricorne. George has a tennis date this afternoon, and Bess and I want to get in some sight-seeing today."

"Of course. I understand," Mimi said. "I don't know how long I'll be tied up with the investigators. Then I have the meeting with Christophe this afternoon. So I'm not sure when I'll be back."

"One more question," Nancy said. "Do you know whether Claude is a member of Le Tricorne?"

"I'm sure he isn't," Mimi answered. "I doubt that someone with a criminal history would ever be asked to join. I can check with William, if you like."

"That might be a good idea. Thanks." Nancy, Bess, and George went upstairs and changed clothes. Bess slipped on a simple green dress and flats. George pulled on slacks and a brown striped shirt, and she packed her tennis clothes and gear in her sports bag. Nancy opted for her blue slacks and a white sweater.

They grabbed their backpacks and left the apartment. Nancy checked one of the maps Mimi had given them, and planned her route.

"We'll go to Le Tricorne first," Nancy said. "It's

not far from the old opera house. We'll get there quicker with the Métro," she declared, "and we can pick up our own *Visite* cards."

They left the island by walking across the Pont Marie and then walked to the Métro stop. Black iron scrollwork surrounded the entrance. They walked down two flights of steps, purchased *Visite* cards, and boarded the train. A map inside the subway car showed them clearly how many stops to watch for until theirs: the Opéra stop.

At the end of the ride, they left the train car, walked up two flights of steps, and came back out into the Paris sunlight. Ahead of them was the ornate Garnier opera house.

"Oooooh, that's where the phantom of the opera lived," Bess reminded the others.

"We've already got our hands full with our own phantom," Nancy said, smirking at Bess.

They walked along the Rue de la Paix for a few blocks, then turned into a narrow side street. In the middle of the block, Nancy spotted a small stained glass window above an old carved door. The colored glass formed the logo of Le Tricorne: the three-cornered hat.

A doorman held the door for them. Inside, three steps led up to a small desk. Behind it sat a middle-aged man. It looked as if he was there to greet those coming in. Nancy knew his real job was to screen people, though, to make sure that only members or their guests made it past him.

Nancy walked decisively to the desk. "I'm Hannah Gruen," she said in French. "We're meeting William Smythe."

The man behind the desk smiled and nodded. Nancy and her friends followed him into a large two-story lounge. A stone fireplace filled one wall. Plush sofas and leather wing chairs formed conversation areas around the room. A few people sat, talking. Others strolled through the lounge into the restaurant beyond.

Nancy nonchalantly walked around the room, looking at the paintings on the walls and the bronze statues on the tables. Bess and George followed her lead.

Finally, they sat down at a game table in the corner. "Nice job getting us in here," Bess said. "I wonder if Hannah's ears are burning."

For a few seconds, Nancy pictured Hannah Gruen in her mind. A warm-hearted woman in her sixties, Hannah had been hired by Nancy's father as a housekeeper after Nancy's mother died.

"Did you notice that these are all over the place?" George said, pocketing a matchbox like the one they'd seen at the theater.

Nancy nodded. "So anyone who's ever been here," she said, "or knows someone who has, could pick up one of these matchboxes." She grabbed a few of the little boxes from the dark, polished table next to her chair and dropped them into her backpack.

Next Nancy leafed through a stack of magazines—issues of the monthly periodical of the club. Most of them were written in French, but a couple were printed in English for the London affiliate chapter of Le Tricorne. Nancy skimmed through them.

"Hmmm, this is interesting," she said, showing them a photo. "When members have done something special, the club honors them with a solid gold matchbox, complete with the Le Tricorne logo."

"Just what everyone needs," George said, rolling her eyes.

Nancy surreptitiously tucked the English magazines and some membership information and rules into her backpack.

"Just what are we doing here exactly?" Bess wondered. She wanted to get on with her day.

"Just wanted to check the place out," Nancy said. "We can leave now. Let's go have lunch at Pascal's."

They rushed quickly past the front desk and out the door of Le Tricorne. After checking the map, they headed back to the Métro, which whisked them underneath the city to the Left Bank.

Pascal's was located in an area once frequented by famous Parisian writers, artists, and musicians. It was still a bustling, noisy area, but now was mostly visited by tourists. Pascal's was very busy, so Nancy and her friends got in line for a table. Although there were tables on the sidewalk along the front of the restaurant, Nancy wanted to go inside.

Finally they were seated, and a passing waiter placed some menus on their table. As Bess and George tried to decide what they wanted, Nancy looked around the room. "Someone who works here dropped a paycheck stub at an arson scene," she muttered. "Who? And why was this person in Mimi's storage room?"

Nancy's eyes scanned the room. She did a double take the instant she recognized a face.

"What is it, Nancy?" Bess asked, craning her head to follow Nancy's gaze. "What do you see?"

Nancy nodded toward a young blond waiter smoothly balancing a tray of soup bowls.

"Wait a minute," George said when she spotted the waiter. "He looks familiar. I've seen him before—but where?"

"On a poster in the lobby of the Musée des Marionettes," Nancy said. "He's Mimi's former assistant, Quentin DuBos!"

5

Dance, Esmeralda, Dance!

Nancy watched Quentin DuBos maneuver through the web of tightly packed tables at Pascal's. After he disappeared into the kitchen, she turned back to Bess and George.

"Nancy, it must have been Quentin's pay stub that you found," Bess said.

"Maybe," Nancy said.

"Well, if so, this isn't much of a mystery," George said. She unrolled a red-and-blue striped napkin and draped it over her jeans. "Maybe he had a part-time job here at the same time that he worked for Mimi. He had total access to the storage room, so he could have dropped the pay stub anytime."

"A good guess, George," Nancy said. "But remember, the pay stub wasn't scorched, and the items around it were. That's why I think it might have been dropped during or after the fire."

When Quentin DuBos came back out of the kitchen, Nancy gestured to him to come over to their table. He opened his order book and looked at her, barely smiling. He had huge blue eyes and sandy blond hair. He didn't say anything.

"Hey, I've seen you before," Nancy said to Quentin. "Didn't you used to work at that puppet theater on Île Saint-Louis?"

"Yeah," he said. The suggestion of a smile disappeared.

"So when did you start working here?" she asked casually.

"Two weeks," he answered. "I'm here two weeks now. What would you like to order?" His English was clipped and precise.

"Mmmm," Nancy scanned her menu quickly.

"I'll have the *soupe au pistou* and a soda," George said, filling in the awkward silence. "Vegetable soup," she said to Bess with a smile. "I'll be a lean, mean tennis machine this afternoon."

Bess and Nancy ordered platters of assorted meats and cheeses, and Quentin left for the kitchen.

"He's really cute," Bess said.

"Yeah, and maybe an arsonist," George added.

"If he dropped that pay stub after he stopped working at the theater," Nancy wondered, "what

39

would he have been doing in the storage room? He didn't work there anymore."

After lunch, George left for her tennis date. Nancy and Bess set off to check out the new shops and boutiques along the Champs Elysées.

George was waiting for them when they got back to the apartment. It was six fifteen. "So you bought out Paris," she observed, helping Bess carry her packages to the table.

"Wait till you see what I got," Bess exclaimed, pulling her new clothes out of the bags and draping them on her bed.

When they heard Mimi in the apartment below, Nancy decided to go down and see how her meeting with Christophe went. "Come in, it's open," Mimi called out when Nancy knocked.

Mimi was sitting at the table. "How was it?" Nancy asked, although she could tell by Mimi's face: She had been crying.

"Oh, Nancy, it's worse than I thought," Mimi said. "My financial situation is very grave. For the first time, I really must consider selling my business."

"I'm so sorry, Mimi," Nancy said. "I know that is very sad news for you."

"Christophe assures me he will keep it going, but when I look around his office, it's hard to believe. He is crazy about real-estate deals and developing wonderful old Parisian properties into flashy new commercial ventures."

"But William vouches for Christophe, and he seems to be a friend," Nancy pointed out, fishing for more information.

"Yes, of course he does," Mimi said. "William was there for our meeting this afternoon. He means well, but Christophe is his partner. Perhaps William is blind to what the truth is about him."

"How long have you known William?" Nancy asked. "And how long have he and Christophe been partners?"

"I met William in London several years ago," Mimi said. "He's from there. I was on vacation, and a mutual friend introduced us. Then when William moved to Paris three years ago to join Christophe as a law partner, he looked me up. William and I have been good friends ever since. He helped me untangle some complicated tax problems regarding my family's estate. He specializes in estate law, and Christophe in property law."

Estate law, Nancy thought. *That gives him access to the family's legal history. Could he have stumbled onto the whereabouts of Mimi's inheritance and be pressuring her to sell so that he and Christophe can get the treasure? Was it William or Christophe who left the matchbox from Le Tricorne at the arson site?*

"Hello? May we come in?" Bess's lilting voice called out from the door to Mimi's apartment.

Mimi brushed the tears from her eyes with the back of her hand and stood up. "Yes, of course," she answered. "Please come in."

"We're starving," George said. "Bess and I want to check out that new salsa club in the Marais district. But we want to get something quick to eat first."

"I'm going to Chèz Sylvie again," Mimi said. "I'd love to have you join me."

"Sounds good to me," Nancy said. "I love sitting outside and watching the people."

The four went down to double check the theater. A carpenter had already repaired the storage-room doors—the one leading to the alley, and the one leading to the backstage area. Mimi wanted to make sure that all was secure.

The marionette that Claude had apparently knocked down was sitting on the wood bench backstage. The doll was a beautiful likeness of a gypsy woman in a flowing white organza dress and was holding a tambourine. "She's so beautiful," Bess said, picking up the crosspieces that controlled the puppet.

"That's Esmeralda," Mimi said. "You know, the gypsy dancer who Quasimodo rescues in *The Hunchback of Notre-Dame*." Mimi showed Bess how to move the strings so that Esmeralda's head, arms, and legs moved.

"You're a natural, Bess," Mimi said while Bess took a turn with the marionette. "If you all decide to come to the fair with me this weekend, I might have you work Esmeralda. That is, if I'm still in business by then. . . ."

Bess tenderly folded the marionette and took it upstairs to their apartment so she could practice later. As the others walked through the theater, Nancy told Mimi about seeing Quentin DuBos waiting tables at Pascal's.

"A waiter?" Mimi said. "How sad. He's such a good puppeteer. I'm sorry he isn't doing that anymore. Wait a minute. . . . No! Do you think it was *his* paycheck stub here in the storage room? Quentin was here?"

"There were some identifying numbers on the paper," Nancy pointed out. "After some investigation the police should be able to determine exactly whose paycheck it was."

"But it must be Quentin!" Mimi said. "The fire examiner agreed with you that it was dropped after the fire, or by someone leaving before it spread. How could he have done it? I knew he was angry when I asked him to work part-time. But I had no idea he could be so vengeful."

"Let's wait until we hear from the investigators," Nancy said. "Then we'll have some concrete answers."

Bess hurried down the stairs to join them. "I'm ready," she announced.

"Good, let's go," George said. "I'm starved—it's almost seven, and I haven't had anything to eat since lunch at Pascal's."

"You get a head start," Mimi said. "I left my purse in the museum. I'll catch up in a minute."

Nancy, Bess, and George left the building and started up the tiny narrow street toward Chèz Sylvie. They hadn't gone more than a few yards when they heard Mimi's voice.

"Nancy!" she called. "Come back—quick! Joan of Arc is gone! She's been kidnapped!"

6

Oh, Non!

"Kidnapped?" Nancy repeated as she ran back to the museum. "What do you mean?"

"She's gone," Mimi cried, showing Nancy the empty display case. "Napoleon, too." The glass case was shattered, and Mimi's two oldest, most prized marionettes were gone.

"Nancy, they've been stolen," Bess said in a hushed voice.

"Yes, stolen," Mimi said. "They are like my babies, though. I think of them as being kidnapped."

Nancy looked around the room. She signaled to the others to be quiet. It was dark in the museum because large heavy shades were pulled down over the windows. Only narrow planes of sunlight crept around the shades and shot across the room. It didn't look or sound as if an intruder was still there, but Nancy crept over to the arch leading to the second room of the museum. She peered around the corner, but the next room was empty.

"We should call the police," Nancy said firmly.

"I'll call William," Mimi decided. "He will call the police." She raced to the phone behind the small desk in the corner of the room.

"Were those two the only ones taken?" Nancy asked Mimi when she returned.

"I think so." The four looked around the two medium-size rooms of the museum. Joan of Arc and Napoleon were the only missing marionettes.

Nancy checked the front door. She couldn't see any signs of a break-in.

William and the policeman arrived at the same time. It was one of the same policemen who had been there earlier that morning.

"Do not say anything," William advised Mimi. Then he turned to the policeman. "Mademoiselle Loiseau is represented by legal counsel," he said. "Me. If you have any questions, please direct them to me."

"But, William . . ." Mimi started to protest.

"Come with me, my dear," William said. He took her elbow and steered her toward the little desk. Nancy watched their animated conversation, then they both returned. The reporting of the theft was awkward from that moment on. The policeman had to ask Mimi questions by asking William, who would then consult quietly with Mimi. Then William would report her answers to the policeman.

Nancy tried to overhear the murmurings between William and Mimi, but without much success.

After the policeman got the basic theft report, he examined the display case and surrounding area. Then he followed Nancy's original path, first checking out the other room of the museum, then the front door. He also checked the locks of the six tall windows in each room.

William reminded the policeman that Nancy and the others had discovered Mimi's cousin at the arson scene earlier. He mentioned Claude's criminal history and suggested that the policeman question him about this theft.

Finally, the policeman flipped his notebook shut and asked that Mimi not leave Paris in the near future. With a thin smile and a nod, he left. William escorted him out.

Mimi turned immediately to Nancy. "This is terrible," she said. "William insisted I not speak directly because *I'm* a suspect!

"Of stealing your own marionettes?" George asked. "I don't get it!"

"No, no, of the arson," Mimi explained. "They told William they had found out I was having financial problems. They suspect I might have set the fire to get some insurance money. How could they possibly think that?"

"Oh, Mimi, I'm so sorry," Bess said. "But don't worry—Nancy will get this figured out. Won't you, Nancy?"

Nancy nodded. "I'll do my best—you can count on that."

After the policeman and William left, Nancy, Bess, George, and Mimi walked down to Chèz Sylvie as they'd originally planned. They took Mimi's usual table at the edge of the sidewalk, just a few yards from the Pont Saint-Louis.

After placing their order, George began telling the others about her tennis match. She pulled her arm across her left shoulder to demonstrate a winning backhand. As she swung back across her body, her fist landed a blow to the midsection of Quentin DuBos.

"Ummmph," Quentin said, drawing his palm up to cradle his waist. He spoke in French, but Nancy understood what he said, and she translated softly for Bess and George: "You've sent yet another assassin to mug me, Mimi." He leaned against the chair briefly, but then he smiled and stood straight. George apologized.

"I'm fine," he said. "I just have to be more on guard, I suppose."

"Quentin, what are you talking about?" Mimi asked. "Assassins . . . mugging . . . on guard? You're not making any sense."

"I'm talking about *her,*" he responded loudly, pointing to Nancy. Then he directed his steady gaze at Bess. "And her," he continued. "And now her," he said with a final glare at George.

"Sit down," Mimi said. "And lower your voice. You're making a scene." Nancy looked around. Several people at the other tables were watching Quentin and Mimi.

Quentin took a seat at Mimi's table. Then he rocked back in his chair and folded his arms defiantly across his chest.

"Now, tell me what you're talking about," Mimi insisted. "And if you're going to talk about my friends, speak English so they can understand."

"I'm talking about being stalked at work," Quentin said tersely. "Being asked questions about my employment by perfect strangers—whom I now suspect were doing so under your orders, no? It is no coincidence that I find you dining with investigators, I'm sure. What I don't understand is this: if you want to know something, why don't you ask me yourself?"

"All right, I will," Mimi said, leaning across the table. "Why did you set fire to my theater?"

Quentin's pale complexion flushed an angry red, and he rocked forward onto all four chair legs with a loud clunk. "What? You can't be . . . how could you . . . ? I can't believe . . ." After these halting phrases in English, Quentin launched into a long tirade in French, most of which Nancy couldn't understand.

Finally he calmed down and looked intently into Mimi's eyes. "I heard about your fire," he said, returning to English. "You know I would never harm that theater—or you, for that matter. I was nowhere near Île Saint-Louis last night."

"You were not only on the island," Nancy said, trying to trap him, "you were in the theater—and left something that we could trace to you."

"Don't be absurd," he said. "I left nothing. I was extremely careful not to—"

Quentin's face reddened again, but this time there was no tirade. He concentrated his gaze on Mimi, avoiding Nancy's eyes. "All right, I was there," he said. "I missed you, and I missed working with the marionettes. I was just going to come by and stand in the wings to watch the show."

Nancy looked around the restaurant again. Most everyone at the surrounding tables had gone back to their own business. One woman at an adjacent table still seemed to be eavesdropping. Nancy stared directly into her eyes, and the woman blinked and looked away.

"I must have gotten to the theater just after the firemen left," Quentin continued, "but I could still smell the smoke. I came in the stage door, but no one was backstage, so I followed my nose to the storage room. I was horrified by the damage, but was afraid to hang around. We had such a fight when I left, remember?" Quentin looked straight at Mimi. "Someone might suspect me of setting the fire for revenge."

Nancy looked at Mimi, assessing her reaction. "Please, Mimi, you know me," Quentin said. "You know I would not do this."

"I believe you," Mimi said, lowering her eyes. But Nancy was not so sure.

Quentin stayed at the table and ordered onion soup and tea. As they ate, Mimi told Quentin about the pay stub he had dropped. He was surprised—he hadn't realized it had been missing.

After a strained silence, George resumed her tennis match report. Nancy noticed the woman at the adjacent table glancing their way again. She caught Nancy's eye and smiled sheepishly. Finally she got up and walked over.

"I'm sorry to bother you, but I can't resist," the woman said. She spoke English, but with a slightly different French accent than Mimi. She was tall and slim, with long, wavy, coppery red hair. "I couldn't help but overhear that your name is Mimi and that you have something to do with puppets. You aren't by chance Mimi Loiseau, are you?"

"I am," Mimi said. She stared at the woman with a puzzled expression. She looked as if she sort of recognized her.

"You're not going to believe this, but I'm Patrice Gerard," the stranger said.

An astounded look came over Mimi's face. Then she jumped up. "Patrice? I don't believe it!"

The two women exchanged brief cheek kisses, then Patrice retrieved a cup of coffee from her table and squeezed her chair between Mimi and George.

"I was going to come by the theater tomorrow," Patrice said. "I just got in this morning and still have jet lag. I was so hoping you and the puppets were still here."

"Patrice and I were classmates at Madame Claire's School for Young Girls here on the Île," Mimi said. "There were eight girls in our set, and we did everything together. That was a million years ago!"

"Seventeen years to be exact," Patrice said. "When we were ten, my father was transferred to Montreal."

"And she might as well have dropped off the face of the earth," Mimi told the others. "We haven't seen or talked to each other since." She turned to Patrice. "What are you doing now? You were going to be a world-famous gymnast, as I remember. You were so talented."

"I competed through college," Patrice said. "But I graduated as a historian. I'm here to write a history of Île Saint-Louis—from its earliest ancient tribal settlements, to now."

"How wonderful!" Nancy said. "This is such a charming part of Paris."

"Where are you staying?" Mimi asked Patrice. "On the island, I trust."

"I'm renting a small room not far from the theater, as a matter of fact," Patrice answered. "Once I figure out how long I'll need to be here, I might try to find something a little bigger."

"I'm getting dessert," Bess announced. "Anyone else interested?"

"Not me," Patrice said, taking her last sip of coffee and then standing. "Mimi, it was wonderful seeing you again. I want to interview you for the book."

"Come by anytime," Mimi said. "I'm usually at the theater or the museum."

"I have to go too," Quentin said. "I start my shift in twenty minutes. Mimi, you know I'm innocent. You *know* that." He turned and began jogging across the bridge to the Left Bank.

"Well, I can always use a little *tarte tatin*," Nancy said. All four ordered the luscious upside-down apple tart, topped with Chèz Sylvie's famous vanilla ice cream. After dinner, they headed back to Mimi's building. Nancy, Bess, and George planned to change their clothes before going out for the night.

As soon as they got to the building, Nancy felt an

eerie sensation across her upper back. It was tickly and itchy, like spiders crawling along her shoulder blades. "Let's check the museum before we go up," she suggested casually. Mimi unlocked the door and switched on the light. They all strolled through the two rooms. Nothing had changed since they had left earlier.

They left the museum, and Mimi locked up. But Nancy couldn't shake the creepy feeling. She led Mimi over to the theater side of the first floor.

"Just the thought of someone stealing your marionettes makes me mad," Bess said to Mimi. "I'm going on upstairs. I want to make sure Esmeralda's okay."

Mimi unlocked the door to the theater and stepped inside. George followed her. Nancy started to take a step, but a noise outdoors nabbed her attention. Cautiously, she walked down the hall to the door leading to the small courtyard at the side of Mimi's building.

She opened the door. Fragrant waves from the garden filled her nostrils. A quaint, old-fashioned pole lamp in the courtyard's far corner illuminated the entire garden. Nancy stepped onto the old cobblestones and walked toward the small fountain in the center. A thumping noise from above drew her attention to the open window in their third-floor apartment.

She heard another thump from the apartment. Her skin stopped itching and tickling—instead it started to feel cold and wet.

Framed in the window of their apartment was Bess's face, scrunched into a frightened look. When she saw Nancy in the courtyard, Bess opened her mouth to say something.

But the words never came out. Something yanked her back inside.

7

Where the Candle Goes Out . . .

"Bess!" Nancy yelled when she saw her friend get pulled back from the open window of their third-floor apartment. "Hold on, we're on our way."

Nancy streaked back into the building and bolted up the stairway. "George, come on," she yelled as she ran. "Bess is in trouble!"

Taking the steps two at a time, Nancy and George were on the third floor in seconds. The two girls roared into their apartment, just in time to see someone dart toward the window. The figure was dressed in all black, but a clump of white dangled from the left hand.

Nancy rushed to Bess, who lay crumpled on the floor. "I'm okay," she moaned as she sat up, rubbing her arm.

Nancy then joined George at the window. "There he goes," George said, pointing into the distance. Like something out of an old movie, the figure in black vaulted from rooftop to rooftop across the Île Saint-Louis.

"What happened?" Mimi said, running into the room. "I was in the theater when I suddenly realized no one else was with me. Then I heard shouts and you two running up the stairs." She looked at Nancy and George, a concerned look on her face.

Nancy explained what she had seen from the courtyard and what she and George had discovered when they arrived at the apartment.

"Sounds like a cat burglar," Mimi said, clearly disturbed.

"Call the police," Nancy called back to Mimi. "And please, stay with Bess until we get back. Come on, George."

Nancy sped out of the building and into the courtyard. She and George dashed in and out of the narrow streets of Île Saint-Louis, looking for the figure dressed in black. Periodically, they would climb an outdoor staircase and scan the horizon. Finally Nancy had to admit they had lost their quarry.

Dejected, she and George hurried back to the apartment. As they turned up the street leading to Mimi's building, something caught Nancy's eye. "Wait a minute," she said to George. "Look. Look

57

out there. Do you see that . . . there, on the river?"

George followed Nancy's gaze and squinted her eyes. Although it was night, the city was bathed in light from streetlamps, candlelit outdoor cafés, and occasional boats bobbing along the Seine.

"There's something out there," George said. "Do you mean that white thing floating on the river?" Just as she spoke, a barge loaded with tourists chugged by, and the clump of white disappeared under the wake. In a few minutes, it bobbed back up, continuing its wavy journey.

"The person who leaped out of Bess's room had something white in his or her left hand," Nancy reminded George.

"Yeah, but that could be anything floating out there," George said. "A piece of paper, a food carton, a loaf of bread . . ."

"Or a marionette," Nancy added.

The two girls turned around, and hurried back to the apartment. Bess was sitting on the small sofa, and Mimi was offering her a cup of hot chocolate.

"Tell me exactly what happened, Bess," Nancy said. "Are you sure you're okay?"

"I'm fine," Bess said. "Just upset." She took a sip of chocolate, then continued. "I came up to make sure the Esmeralda marionette was okay," Bess reminded them. "When I got here, that person was standing right over there." She pointed to the corner with the bookcase and small writing desk.

"Was it a man or a woman?" Nancy asked.

"I couldn't tell," Bess replied. "It all happened so fast. The person was dressed in black sweats and a cap and had a mask over the face."

"What do you mean, a mask?" George asked.

"I mean a *mask*," Bess said, a little impatiently. "You know, like a Halloween mask—a rubbery one that covers your face and chin. It was a sort of grayish, monsterlike face."

"So, what happened when you saw the intruder?" Nancy prompted.

"I tried to get back out of the room, but the person cut me off at the door. That's when I raced to the window. I was going to scream for help, but whoever it was grabbed my arm and wrenched it back. The person then flung me onto the floor, and I sort of lost my breath for a minute or two." She sighed. "Worst of all, Esmeralda is gone!"

"And that's the clump of white we saw the person carrying," Nancy concluded.

A knock on the door announced a policeman—once again. This officer was not the same one who had been there for the arson last night and the theft of the other two marionettes earlier that evening.

"It is probably the burglar we have been tracking for the last several months," the officer said after hearing the story. "Someone has been plaguing our lovely island, but we'll catch him. He wore gloves, did he not?" the policeman asked Bess.

"Yes, and a mask," Bess explained.

"Ah, the mask," the policeman said. "That proves it. The burglar has worn a mask for other thefts too. We are very close to apprehending the suspect, I can tell you that. There is a criminal recently released who seems to be back to his old ways. I'll let you know when we have him in our custody."

The policeman made a few more notes and left.

"Mimi, I am so sorry about Esmeralda," Bess said. "You trusted me with her."

"Please, Bess, do not feel bad. I could not even save my Joan of Arc from being kidnapped," Mimi said in a soft voice.

Over hot chocolate and madeleine cookies, the four hashed over the day's events. Nancy tried to piece together the puppet incidents. "Esmeralda was lying next to Claude when we surprised him in the burned-out storage room," she began. "Then two marionettes were stolen while we were all away from the building."

"Two very valuable ones," Mimi added.

"Right," Nancy agreed. "Finally Esmeralda is stolen while we're at Chèz Sylvie."

"Do you think Claude did all of this?" George asked.

"Or do you buy the policeman's guess that it's some sort of rooftop cat burglar?" Bess wondered.

"It's hard to say," Nancy concluded. "Was Claude in the storage room to steal Esmeralda this morning? And when we surprised him, he just bugged out— but came back tonight to finish the job? We know the *Visite* card was missing after he left the storage room. So did he just come to retrieve that, knocking Esmeralda off her shelf by mistake?"

"But if it was his *Visite* card in the storage room, then it's possible it was he who set the fire, right?" Mimi said.

"Yes, but maybe the fire wasn't the point," Nancy offered. "Maybe he was in the storage room in the first place to steal the marionette, and he set the fire by accident."

"That reminds me," Mimi said. "I asked William whether Claude belonged to Le Tricorne, and he said absolutely not. No one with a criminal record is allowed in, and they check thoroughly."

Sipping the luscious chocolate brew and nibbling her cookie, Nancy got lost in thought for a moment. George reined her back in.

"Tell them what we saw on the Seine, Nancy," George urged.

Nancy described seeing the person on the rooftops grasping a clump of white, then noticing the odd clump of white on the river. "It was almost shapeless. It didn't really look like a box or a piece of wood or paper. It was sort of a blob."

"Like a fluffy white dancing dress?" Bess asked quietly.

"It could be," Nancy said.

"If it is Esmeralda, she will float—at least for a while. Her wooden body is very lightweight, and the dress netting is full enough to provide a lot of buoyancy," Mimi pointed out.

"I know," Bess said, jumping up. "We'll follow the legend—the one in the performance last night. The legend about finding lost things that have gone into the Seine. People in Paris have been using it for three hundred years—it *must* work!"

"I'd like to take a look down there, just in case," Nancy said. That seemed to be all the encouragement Bess needed. She pulled on a red sweater, grabbed a fat round candle from the table, found a baguette near the refrigerator and tore off a piece, and started out the door. "Come *on!*" she commanded.

"I'll get a piece of wood from backstage," Mimi said. They all went downstairs.

"Nancy has her notebook and a pen, I'm sure," George said, smirking at her friend. "She never leaves home without it."

"Wait a minute," Bess said. "Let's go over the legend and make sure we haven't forgotten anything."

"The seeker must write the name of the lost object

on a piece of paper and wrap it around a hunk of bread," Nancy recalled.

"Then we put that on a plank of wood, along with a candle," Mimi added.

"We light the candle and float the plank on the Seine," George said.

"And wherever the candle goes out, that's where the lost item will be found," concluded Bess.

They gathered up all the items and walked to the bank of the Seine near where Nancy had spotted the floating white clump. As they walked, shadows— shadows which were not their own—seemed to be following them. Twice, Nancy turned quickly, but the shadows seemed to melt into the black spaces between the buildings.

Finally they reached the river. They hurried down the stone steps at the end of the bridge to the cobblestone walkway along the edge of the water. The river was dark, choppy, and so high that it occasionally spilled over the cobblestones and lapped at the legs of a bench sitting on the walk.

In the distance, Emmanuel tolled midnight. Clouds covered the moon and stars. When the bell was finally quiet, the silence was eerie.

Bess dripped some candle wax on the plank of charred wood from the storage room. Then she secured the base of the candle to the melted wax.

Nancy wrote MIMI'S MARIONETTE, ESMERALDA on the piece of paper, tied it to a piece of bread with a ribbon Mimi handed her, and placed it on the plank.

Nancy felt a rush of anticipation, and a shiver cascaded down her spine. She turned and looked around them and then back up the steps to the street—but she didn't see anyone. Still, she couldn't shake the feeling that they were being watched.

Bess pushed the loaded plank into the Seine. At first it looked as if it would float right back into her hands. But then it caught a small wave. Bobbing and teetering, the candle stayed lit as the plank headed farther down the river.

Never taking her eyes from the candle flame, Nancy watched the plank dip and crest as it moved farther away. Then it took a lurching turn and headed toward the other bank, finally bumping into the cobblestones directly across the river.

The plank and its cargo were swallowed up in dark shadows. Nancy could see only the candle flame as it flickered and then went out.

"Come on," she said, racing up the stone stairway, across the bridge, and back down the stairway to the river's edge on the opposite bank.

Nancy was the first to arrive at the bottom of the steps and the first to see Esmeralda. The doll had washed up onto the shiny slick stones. A large hole was gouged into the back of its head, and its body was ripped down the spine. The sickening sight made the hairs on the back of Nancy's arms spike up with a clammy chill. Right at that moment she heard someone in the shadows beneath the stone stairway sip a tiny breath of air.

8

Excusez-moi!

Nancy froze, stifling the shiver that tried to rush through her. She strained her eyes, looking hard into the shadows underneath the stone steps. Like slow-motion animation, a dark form began to take shape.

"Esmeralda!" Bess's cry broke Nancy's focus. She turned to see Bess bouncing down the stairway, and toward the marionette. At the same moment, the figure beneath the steps rushed past Nancy, slamming her down on the wet cobblestone walkway.

Nancy got to her feet in time to see the person barrel up the steps, shoving George and Mimi into the stone wall and out of the way.

Nancy clambered up the steps, joining George in the chase. But by the time they reached the bridge, the person was gone.

Bess and Mimi joined them on the bridge. "Did anyone see who it was?" Mimi asked. "It all happened so fast, I didn't get a good look at the guy."

"It probably wouldn't matter if you did," Nancy said. "The person was wearing a mask—some sort of a monster face."

"That's the one, I'll bet," Bess said. "The one who stole Esmeralda."

"I thought someone was following us all along," Nancy said. "Maybe that was who it was."

"Should we call the police?" Mimi said.

"Maybe we should just have an officer with us all the time," George said with a crooked smile. "Then we wouldn't have to call every hour or so."

"We have nothing to report this time," Nancy said. "Someone hid when I came down, ran when Bess cried out, and wore a mask. Not exactly crimes."

"But what about knocking you down and pushing us into the wall?" Mimi asked.

"Those could easily be called accidents," Nancy said. "The person could have been scared of *us* and was trying to get away."

They walked home quickly, Bess carrying the damaged, waterlogged Esmeralda. Back in their apartment, the three friends discussed their plans for the next day. George had another tennis match, and Bess wanted to go to the Musée d'Orsay. "They have the most wonderful bronze statues there. All by Dégas. Ballerinas, of course."

"I'm going to call Christophe in the morning," Nancy said. "I'd like to ask him a few questions. Maybe I can tell him I want to talk about some property here on the island and set up a meeting tomorrow."

"After the museum, I'm going shopping," Bess said. "How about we try one of the famous Parisian flea markets? If you're interested, meet me at the Marché aux Puces. It's the most famous one, and I hear you can get designer boots at unbelievable prices! I'll be there from noon to whenever."

Everyone thought that sounded good and agreed to meet. Nancy soon fell into bed, again falling asleep with Juliette's journal.

On Wednesday morning Nancy woke at about eight o'clock. She had had a dream about working on a large jigsaw puzzle with missing pieces. *There was something about a puzzle in Juliette's journal*, she thought. She picked up the book, which was still lying open near her pillow. "Where was it . . . oh, here it is." Not quite awake yet, Nancy reread the entry.

The day it was written, Juliette had received some custom items ordered from a leather worker named Jacques Guerin. In her journal she raved about the man's artistry and craftsmanship. Then she wrote the lines Nancy had remembered in her dream.

I feared that he would not be able to under-
stand my simple drawing, but he is a true artist.
He has perfectly executed my design. Now the
puzzle is complete.

Nancy closed the book and made her bed. After her shower, she called Christophe and told him she'd like to meet with him. She said she represented her father, who was interested in setting up a partnership to invest in some property on the island. Christophe asked her to come to his office at one o'clock.

After dressing in black slacks and a crisp white shirt, Nancy went downstairs to check on Mimi.

"Ah, I was just going to call you," Mimi said. "I'm getting ready to go out. One of the *bouquinistes*—a bookstall owner—found a book I was looking for. Would you like to shop a little with me this morning?" She wore a deep red jacket and pants that matched her lipstick.

"Sure," Nancy said.

Nancy and Mimi walked over the bridges to the *quais*—the lanes where the bookstalls were located. "I need to get there when the *bouquiniste* is there," Mimi said. "They all set their own hours, and their schedules aren't always the same every day."

"Until I actually saw these bookstalls, I had pictured the whole operation differently," Nancy said. "I thought they brought their books and stalls in every

69

day and set them up for business. I'm surprised to see that the stalls are actually attached to the railing."

"Oh, yes. And every night, the *bouquinistes* just close the bins and lock them up. The books stay inside until the *bouquiniste* returns."

In just a few minutes they reached the Quai Saint Michel. Before them stretched blocks and blocks of bookstalls. Behind them loomed the huge presence of Notre-Dame. Farther down the Seine on the opposite bank stood the Louvre. They strolled past a few booksellers, and then one that sold old maps and other geographical prints. Two or three merchants in a row specialized in postcards and old letters. One sold photographs and drawings.

Mimi walked straight to the merchant who held her book. After a little bargaining, Mimi handed over her money and received the book.

"I'm so thrilled to finally get this," she said, opening it immediately. She showed Nancy the title page. It was a history of European puppetmakers, printed in the early 1900s. "Look," she said, turning to one of the middle chapters. Pages and pages were devoted to her family.

Mimi scanned the pages quickly. "Good," she said. "It's all here. Sometimes a really old book has lost pages." She passed the book to Nancy. "I used to have a wonderful copy of this. It was a first edition and was even autographed by the author with a special inscription to my great-grandmother. But recently I misplaced it. This will never take the place of that edition, but it will have to do."

Nancy quoted from Juliette's journal: "I was always fascinated by the Egyptians because they were buried in pyramids and surrounded by mysteries and clues." Then Nancy told Mimi about the journal entry that mentioned a puzzle.

"She must have been talking about Jacques Guerin, the man who crafted many of the backdrops and sets that I still use today. See, that's what I mean about her," Mimi said. "She loved mysteries and puzzles. It is very easy for me to believe she has somehow hidden a family treasure for me to find."

They strolled along the *quais* for a couple of hours, checking out not only the bookstalls, but also a few shops on the other side of the walk. When Emmanuel tolled eleven thirty, Mimi put down the box of postcards she had been scanning. "Patrice called this morning and asked me to meet her for an early lunch. If you don't have plans, come join us. The café is on the next block."

Nancy had an hour and a half before she met with Christophe, and she had pretty much skipped breakfast. So she walked with Mimi to the restaurant. She had decided not to tell her friend just yet that she was meeting Christophe. *I'd better wait and see if I have something interesting to report,* she told herself.

71

Patrice was waiting for them at the café. She was dressed in a purple suit that contrasted drastically with her red hair. The three of them ordered soup, salad, and lemonade. Then Patrice and Mimi began talking about their families and catching each other up on what had happened to them over the past several years.

"So when will your next performance be?" Patrice asked Mimi. "I can't wait to see one. I remember my mother bringing me to see your parents' shows when I was a child."

"I'm not sure," Mimi said. "To tell you the truth, things are not going well with the theater. I really don't want to go into it now, but I'm considering selling the property."

"Oh, no," Patrice said. She had large green eyes that flashed with flecks of gold. "I'm so sorry to hear that. I know you must have very mixed feelings. Is that what Quentin meant last night when he said he missed being there? I overheard him saying something like this at the café. I gathered he used to work at the theater, but doesn't now?"

Mimi explained why Quentin had left, and then she told Patrice about her commitment to the charity fund country fair the coming weekend. "Nancy, I haven't had a chance to tell you this yet, but I called Quentin this morning and asked him if he'd be interested in working for me on Saturday and Sunday at the fair. He turned me down. He didn't say why."

"Well, Bess and George and I talked it over, and we'd be happy to do what we can to help," Nancy said.

"Are you sure?" Mimi asked. "I don't want to interfere with your vacation."

"It'll be fun," Nancy said. "Something different to do."

"Wonderful! Thank you so much," Mimi said. "I have William to thank for the job. He's the attorney for the charity organization. We hoped it might bring me some publicity and increase my business—but it may be too late for that. Anyway, I'll try to give you plenty of free time so you can enjoy the festivities."

"Is there anything I can do?" Patrice offered. "I haven't touched a marionette for twenty years, but I remember some of the things you taught me when we were kids."

"I can use all the hands I can get," Mimi said. "I wasn't given any restrictions on the number of puppeteers I could bring, so consider yourself part of the troupe."

"Are you doing *Hunchback,* by any chance?" Patrice asked. "That's the story I remember the best. As a matter of fact, I'm going to the Panthéon after lunch—you two ought to come."

"The Panthéon is a large tomb where the ashes of many great Parisians are buried," Mimi explained.

"And I take it since we were talking about *The Hunchback of Notre-Dame*, that its author is buried there?" Nancy guessed.

"Yes—Victor Hugo," Patrice said. "One of the greats."

Time passed quickly as they ate and talked. Nancy checked her watch and was surprised to see that it was already 12:35. "Whoa, I'd better get going," she said. "I have lots to do this afternoon." She left money for her share of the lunch, said good-bye to the two women, and left.

Nancy took the Métro to Christophe's office, which was near the old opera house—not far from Le Tricorne. When she arrived, the receptionist took her into an elegant conference room. It smelled like old leather and fresh oil paintings. She placed Christophe's day planner on the table opposite Nancy's chair and told her that Christophe would be fifteen minutes late.

After the receptionist left, Nancy walked quickly around to the other side of the table. She stood with her back to the table and Christophe's day planner. Pretending to look at the painting on the wall, she reached back and knocked the day planner to the floor.

She dove to the floor and began quickly scanning

through his appointments and meeting schedules. She soon came across her own name written in a crisp script. After her appointment was another notation. SSUL LOFT, 3P. But it was the name following those words that took her breath away. "C. Loiseau," she whispered. "C . . . Claude, maybe? Is Christophe meeting with Claude Loiseau?"

She was so surprised by her discovery that she didn't hear the door quietly open and shut.

She finally realized she wasn't alone when she saw, out of the corner of her eye, two highly polished men's shoes coming toward her.

"You must be Miss Drew," said a low voice with a heavy French accent.

9

Stakeout at Saint-Sulpice

"And you are Mr. Binet," Nancy said, standing quickly. She handed over his day planner. "I bumped the table, and this fell off." Then she extended her hand. "How nice of you to meet me on such short notice. As I said, I'm only in town for a short time."

Christophe shook her hand briefly, then gestured for her to sit down.

"My partner, William Smythe, tells me you and your friends are staying in Mimi Loiseau's guest apartment," he began, "and that your father is Carson Drew. I believe I've heard of him. Is that possible?"

"He represents a group that would like to invest in some commercial property in Paris. We thought that you, as a specialist in property law, might know what's available. Or you at least would be able to direct us to the right realtor."

"I can certainly give you a list of some brokers and some properties that might be of interest," Christophe responded. "Do they want any particular types of business, or areas of the city?"

"Actually, I understand that Mimi's property could be on the market soon," Nancy said. "That would be just about what they're looking for. But I understand that you have a first option there."

"I am very interested in the theater and shop, yes," Christophe said. "If she decides to sell, I can assure you it will go quickly. So your father's group is interested in entertainment or services property?"

"Well, probably not," Nancy said. "They're looking more for office buildings or complexes. But the Loiseau building would be great for that. If they closed the theater and museum and converted the building to—"

"As I said, that property is not available." Christophe interrupted her, then began jotting down some notes. The conversation went on for another half an hour. Nancy persisted in asking him questions that might tell her what his intent was for Mimi's building, but he continued to brush off that subject and talk about other properties. When she realized she was not going to get any more information from him, she thanked him for his help and left.

As soon as she got outside, she found a small park, sat down on a bench, and got out her map. *Christophe's note said "SSul loft,"* she reminded herself. *Where would I find a loft? An apartment or house, a barn, or maybe an art gallery . . . ?* She scanned the map for LOFT, but it was practically impossible to find that short word in the sea of tiny words sprinkled around Paris.

She got out her guidebook and began scanning the index with her finger. "It'll be easier to just follow him," she said out loud to herself, still looking. "Wait a minute. Loft—choir loft." Her finger stopped on these words. "Maybe it's a church!"

She turned to the list of churches in her guidebook. She soon found the word "loft," tucked into the description of *Saint-Sulpice*. This was described by many as one of the largest churches in Paris.

That's got to be it, she told herself. *SSu . . . Saint-Sulpice.* She checked her watch. It was ten minutes past two. She stuffed the map and guidebook in her backpack, took out her *Visite* card, and headed for the nearest Métro station.

She arrived at Saint-Sulpice at about two thirty. The church was huge. A large stone courtyard was anchored in the middle with an enormous fountain.

Nancy climbed dozens of steps to the massive columns supporting the front of the church. *Could Christophe's meeting really be with Claude Loiseau?*

she wondered as she walked through the large wooden doors. *Why would Christophe meet with Mimi's ex-con cousin?*

Inside the church Nancy scanned notices and brochures on a table in the entryway. She found a pamphlet in English, which gave the answer to one of her questions: ORGANIST: CLAUDE LOISEAU.

In a small room to the right of the church's entrance, a large mural by Delacroix covered the wall and ceiling. The main room of the church seemed to extend for yards, and it rose up many stories. Its walls were lined with statues mounted on marble pedestals. Elaborately carved arches and columns led to alcoves and smaller rooms.

Nancy looked around. Hovering over the back of the church was an enormous pipe organ. It was built to look like its own building, with angels and other figures on its roof, and a clock mounted in its front. She quickly found the stairway leading to the choir loft, then crept up the steps.

Nancy was relieved to find that no one was in the loft yet. After a quick check of the room, she found a perfect hiding place, behind a hanging screen that masked some heating equipment in the corner of the loft. She would be able to hear everything, and she could even see a little around the edge of the screen.

They'll probably be talking in French, Nancy reasoned. *Thank goodness for electronics.* She took her handheld tape recorder out of the backpack and checked to make sure it was loaded with batteries and a tape.

Nancy had been tucked behind the screen only a few minutes when Claude arrived. It was 2:45. He fussed around the loft for a while, turning chairs and gathering up music that was laying around. Then he sat down to play. Nancy's whole body vibrated with the sound.

Christophe arrived promptly at three o'clock. Claude kept playing until Christophe tapped him on the shoulder. Then he swung his legs around on the bench to face Christophe.

Although they spoke in French, Nancy was able to understand most of what they said. At first they just exchanged greetings, but Nancy could tell this wasn't the first time they'd met.

Then Christophe's voice took on a commanding tone. "I have told you before to stay away from Mimi," he said. "This will be the last time I mention this."

Claude fired back fast, and Nancy picked up the French words for "cousin" and "family."

The two men argued for several minutes. Their voices grew louder as the argument progressed.

Finally Claude lowered his voice to say something. Nancy didn't get the whole sentence, but she understood the last two words: *"le trésor."* Claude hissed the last word like a striking snake. *Le trésor,* Nancy thought—*the treasure.*

Christophe's tone became even more heated. The two talked furiously about the treasure and Mimi, and Claude used the French word *"heritage."* Nancy knew this meant inheritance. Then Claude mentioned Juliette and the French word *"tombe."*

Christophe spoke harshly one last time and seemed to be warning Claude. When he turned to leave, Nancy moved her position slightly, so she could see around the edge of the screen without being discovered.

As Christophe started down the loft stairway, a flapping, humming sound filled the air. Nancy's breath caught in her throat as she watched two bats flutter past Christophe's head and toward the massive organ keyboards.

Claude yelled something, and swatted at the bats with a piece of sheet music. He was obviously terrified by the dipping and darting creatures. Nancy knew she couldn't make a sound, so she held her position. She turned off the recorder and dropped it into her pack.

From the stairway, Christophe chuckled at Claude. He seemed to enjoy watching Claude try to fight off the bats. Then Nancy heard more footsteps as Christophe continued down the steps. She directed her attention back to the loft.

Claude frantically flailed his arms, but the bats swooped and spun. He jumped off the organ bench, still waving his arms. His movements only seemed to increase the bats' fury. As Nancy watched with alarm, he began shooing the bats toward her corner.

She ducked back against the heating pipe, but it was hot—so she jumped forward again. She bumped the screen, but grabbed it quickly. She was so intent on keeping the screen still and herself hidden that she didn't see the pointy-eared creature fly in to join her. But she definitely felt its little claws land just above her ear.

10

Booked!

Nancy clamped her hand on her mouth to keep from screaming. The bat clung to her hair, its wings fluttering. She could feel its tiny heart beating fast as it rested from its battle with Claude.

"Eeyah!" Claude yelled from the other side of the screen. Nancy's bat darted away. She shook her head and peeked around the screen. She saw only Claude's back as he thundered toward the stairway and disappeared.

Nancy waited about ten minutes; she had to make sure Claude wasn't coming back up. Then she cautiously tiptoed down the stairway and hurried out the front door.

Once outside, she took her first big breath of fresh air in an hour. It was after three o'clock, so she caught a bus to the Marché aux Puces—which translated to "market of fleas"—to meet Bess and George.

It didn't take her long to find Bess, who was poking through a roomful of boots and shoes. "George is checking out sweaters down the row," Bess told her. "So what's been happening with you today?"

"I've got a lot to tell you," Nancy said. "But let's wait until we eat. I want to tell you both at once, and it's a long story." They strolled in and out of the different shops and talked with vendors until they caught up with George. She was watching for them in a small café.

After they all ordered burgers, *pommes frites*, and sodas, Bess turned to Nancy. "Okay," she said, "tell us everything."

"I'm going to start at the end and work backward," Nancy said. She first told them about meeting with Christophe and eavesdropping on his confrontation with Claude. And the bats.

"Bats!" Bess said with a sneer of distaste. "Yuck!"

"They're great," George reminded her. "They eat a lot of bugs—which you *really* don't like."

"But one was on Nancy's *head*!" Bess pointed out. "I still say *yuck*!"

"I didn't hear all of the argument between Claude and Christope," Nancy reported. "But I got enough to know that they were talking about the Loiseau family treasure and Mimi's inheritance from Juliette.

I'll have Mimi translate the tape when we get back to the apartment."

"I just can't see how everything ties together," George said. "Who was behind the arson, and why? Who stole the puppets? Are the two crimes related?"

"We don't know yet," Nancy said. "I don't agree with the police, though, who think the marionettes were stolen by some cat burglar. I have a hunch that most professional burglars don't steal puppets."

"So you think it wasn't just a random theft," Bess said. "Someone targeted the museum."

Nancy nodded as the waiter brought their food. "So did someone steal the puppets because they're valuable, or because they might lead to the treasure?" she wondered.

"Well, they didn't steal Esmeralda for her value," Bess said. "They totally mutilated her. She's not worth much now."

"Exactly," Nancy said. "I believe someone knows about the treasure, and has connected it to the puppets. Maybe they think the treasure, or a clue to the treasure, is hidden *inside* one of the dolls."

"What about Christophe and Claude?" George asked. "Do you think they're working together? Do you suppose William knows about their meeting?"

"Maybe we can answer some of those questions when Mimi translates the tape," Nancy said, "and fills in the blanks."

They stopped talking for a minute to eat. "Yum," Bess declared. "The French sure know how to make French fries!"

After they finished eating, Bess talked them into going to one last shop. "It's full of old jewelry and clothes," she said. "It's a good place to get some souvenirs of our trip—cheap."

The three wandered inside the shop and were greeted by the smiling vendor. While Bess checked out the earrings and George swung some golf clubs, Nancy leafed through a bin of old photographs.

"Whoa, look at this," she said. The face of Juliette Loiseau stared up at her. She was standing by a tree. In the foreground, in a courtyard with a fountain, two men faced off in a duel. Behind Juliette and the tree was a row of three-story houses.

Nancy bought the photo, and she and her friends headed back to Île Saint-Louis. As they crossed the bridge to the island, they spotted Mimi, Quentin, and Patrice at Chèz Sylvie.

"Look at this incredible photograph I got at the flea market," Nancy said.

"I don't believe it," Mimi said. "That is Juliette and her husband, Gilles! It looks like he's fighting a duel."

"Perhaps for the hand of Juliette," Quentin said. "It looks like it was taken at Place des Vosges."

"It probably was," Mimi said. "Juliette's family lived there."

"So did Victor Hugo and his family," Patrice added.

Mimi studied the photo carefully. "But I have never even heard of this," she said. "I've never seen the picture, never heard of a duel. It's amazing—I thought I knew everything about my family."

Nancy decided not to say anything about the argument between Christophe and Claude until she could speak to Mimi alone.

"How long did Juliette live there?" Nancy asked.

"All her life," Mimi answered. "The building where I live was the theater back then, and my father and mother and I lived on the upper two floors. Juliette lived in the Place des Voges until she died."

"And is she buried in Paris?" Nancy asked.

"Yes—in Père-Lachaise cemetery," Mimi said.

When they finished eating, Nancy announced that she wanted to go back to the *quais* and browse the bookstalls for some more old photos of Paris. Everyone else headed for their respective homes.

Nancy crossed back over the bridge. It was dark, and a sudden heavy fog rolled down the Seine and clung to everything. As she walked toward the *quais*, she couldn't shake the feeling that someone was following her—again.

Just then she started to hear footsteps behind her. She stopped, and so did the footsteps. Then she heard breathing behind her, but when she turned, she saw only the pale yellow glow of some street-lamps.

As she walked toward the large bookstall bins perched on the stone walls along the river, she began to wonder if this was such a good idea. *The fog is so thick, the* bouquinistes *are probably all locking up for the night,* she told herself. *But I'm almost there. . . .*

She hurried along. Behind her, she heard another set of quickened steps. Before she could turn around, a sharp pain spread across the back of her head. The pain cascaded to the back of her knees, and she sank to the ground. She could feel consciousness dimming. The foggy gray around her turned black.

When she came to, it was still totally dark. She was lying on a bumpy bed of hard surfaces and sharp corners. When she sat up, she banged her already sore head on a metal ceiling that echoed with a metallic *thwannng.* Cautiously she reached out. Her arm hit an unyielding metal mass. She ran her hand along the hard-cornered blocks under her legs, and the familiar smell of old books filled her nostrils. As she realized where she was, the temperature of her skin seemed to drop twenty degrees. "It's a bookstall," she whispered. "I'm locked in a bookstall."

11

An Eye for an Eye

Nancy fought the panic rising in her throat. Her body felt numb. She shook her head and strained to see in the dark.

Pale gray light seeped through a tiny gap in the seam between the top and bottom of the bin. As she moved around in the tight quarters, the numbness in her limbs began to leave. She flexed her tingling fingers and spread her hands.

A sudden throbbing pain opened up in the back of her head. She felt the site gingerly and discovered a hard little knot of tenderness. She banged on the metal wall with her fist and yelled for help. She heard nothing on the other side of the metal.

She pictured the exterior of a bookstall. The lid was closed down like the lid on a barbecue grill. She remembered that most lids had a heavy metal plate with a narrow cutout, which clamped over an iron loop. A padlock could be slipped through the loop, to lock the top to the bottom. Nancy pushed on the lid. It rocked and clattered, but stayed closed.

She felt around her. "Please, someone be here," she whispered. When she felt the familiar soft drape of her leather backpack, a lump of relief swelled in her throat. She rummaged through the pack, her fingers and brain making familiar connections in the dark.

She pulled out her cell phone and flipped it open. The green glow comforted her. But there was no reception; she couldn't connect with the world outside her metal box. She turned on her penlight. A narrow cylinder of yellow light shot across her lap.

She tried to unkink her legs in the cramped bin, but a sharp edge ripped her slacks and scraped her calf. "Yikes," she cried. "What was that?"

She flashed her light over to the corner of the table. A folded black metal bistro chair lay across the books. The end of one of the thin, curved legs had torn her slacks. Nancy studied the chair.

"Okay, think," she told herself. "Odds are it was not the *bouquiniste* who knocked me out and threw me into the bookstall. Whoever did this had to jimmy the lock to get this stall open. The padlock probably no longer works. Something—a rod or a piece of wood must be jammed through the loop to hold the bin together."

Quickly, Nancy used the screwdriver on her pocketknife to detach one of the thin legs of the folding chair. Then she wedged it through the small gap in the metal. Using a sawing motion, she worked the chair leg along the seam toward the middle of the lid.

At last she felt the chair leg hit something on the outside of the bin. It made a dull thud. She figured a piece of wood or even a rolled-up newspaper or magazine was stuffed through the loop. She kept working the chair leg along until she heard another thud. But this one was different from the one before. Whatever had been wedged into the loop to hold the lid shut had been pushed out, and it had fallen to the ground.

She leaned on the lid, but it still didn't open. She visualized the front of the bin, and realized that the metal plate from the lid was still clamped over the loop on the bottom of the bin. Using the chair leg like a crowbar, she jimmied the plate out and up over the loop. Finally—with a cry of triumph—she pushed open the bookstall lid.

At first her legs were weak and jiggly, but she soon got her bearings. Using a piece of paper to protect fingerprints, she picked up the broken padlock and the piece of wood that she suspected had kept the lid closed. Checking her map, she hurried to the nearest police station. She explained what had happened, and handed over the evidence. An on-site medic looked her over and pronounced her okay.

When she got back to the apartment, Bess, George, and Mimi were pulling on their jackets.

"Nancy!" George cried. "We were just forming a posse to look for you. Where have you been?"

Nancy told them about being locked in the book-stall. Just relating the story made the back of her head throb and her friends gasp.

"Oh, Nancy," Mimi said. She placed her hand on Nancy's arm. "I feel terrible. You wouldn't have been in such danger if it weren't for me. I should never have involved you all."

"Someone must know you're working on the case," Bess said to Nancy. "That's really scary."

Nancy told Mimi about the meeting between Christophe and Claude. Mimi was stunned. "I'm not surprised to hear that William told Christophe about Claude," she said. "But I had no idea they knew each other. I wonder if William knows about this."

"I was curious about that myself," Nancy said. "Could you listen to this tape and fill in what I missed?" Nancy turned on the tape recorder.

Nancy had translated the argument correctly. "At the end, Claude says that the treasure was probably buried with the old lady," Mimi added.

"That's the sentence in which he mentions Juliette

and the word *"tombe,"* right?" Nancy said.

"Yes," Mimi said. She listened until the end of the recording, when Claude began battling the bats. "Christophe warns Claude one last time," Mimi translated, "and adds that if there is a family treasure, Claude has no claim to it."

"It sounds as if Christophe thinks the treasure might not even exist," Nancy said. "Just like William does." She thanked Mimi, who then went down to her apartment.

"Do you have any idea of who locked you in the bookstall, Nancy?" Bess asked. "Just thinking about it makes me nervous."

"No, not yet," Nancy said.

"Well Quentin left our table shortly after you did," George said. "Maybe it was him."

Nancy didn't say anything for a few minutes, and finally Bess broke the silence. "Are you okay, Nancy?" she asked. "You must have felt like you were in a tomb."

"Interesting that you should say that," Nancy said quietly. She walked over and looked out the window. "I kind of feel like Juliette is trying to point us in the right direction. We just have to think like her—think like someone who loves mysteries and clues."

"Well, that shouldn't be too hard for you," George said with a small grin.

"I've been working on another theory about this

case," Nancy said. She quoted the line she had read in Juliette's diary about the artistic leatherworker Jacques Guerin, and how he had completed "the puzzle." Then she shared the sentence from the book Mimi got from the *bouquiniste*. "Juliette said something about Egyptians being buried with lots of mysteries and clues," she told her friends. "And in the choir loft, Claude said that the treasure was probably buried with Juliette."

"What are you thinking?" George asked.

"So far, everyone has been focusing on the puppets to try to find the treasure. What if it doesn't have anything at all to do with the dolls? What if it's something entirely unrelated? Maybe Claude was right. Maybe the clues or even the treasure *was* buried with Juliette—literally."

"So she'd be surrounded by mysteries and clues, like the Egyptians," George concluded.

"Something like that," Nancy said.

"So what's next?" Bess asked.

"First I want to go to Place des Vosges and just take a look around," Nancy said.

"That's where Juliette lived, right?" Bess asked.

"That's right," Nancy said. "Then we might take a tour of Père-Lachaise. It's a very famous cemetery. A lot of celebrities are buried there, and tourists go there all the time."

"Well, that's us," Bess said. "Tourists. I promised

94

to rehearse with Mimi and Patrice tomorrow morning. If I can learn the moves, Mimi might let me work Esmeralda at the fair this weekend. We were able to fix her pretty well. I've been practicing on my own, but I'll feel better if I work with Mimi some more. I'm still having trouble getting Esmeralda to tap her tambourine. But don't go to Père-Lachaise without me."

"Okay, we'll go there later tomorrow. I'll go to Place des Vosges in the morning."

"I'll go with you," George said. "Mimi said the Victor Hugo museum is there, and he's one of my favorite authors." George had a concerned look on her face. "This whole case has taken a dangerous turn," George said. "I'm not liking it, Nancy."

"We just have to be careful," Nancy said. "We all have to stay alert. Someone obviously thinks we're a threat."

"Which must mean that we're close to cracking the case, right?" Bess noted.

"Exactly," Nancy agreed. "Now, if only I could figure out exactly how. . . ."

Even with a headache, Nancy read some more of Juliette's journal before crashing. The last thing she read that night stuck with her:

Tell everyone about the niche—it's in the corner that points to Notre-Dame.

●●●

Nancy awoke with a start on Thursday morning. As she gained consciousness, everything that happened the day before flooded her mind—the argument between Claude and Christophe, the ice cream with Patrice and Quentin, and the horrible feeling of being locked into the bookstall.

After a quick breakfast of croissants and juice in their apartment, Bess left to rehearse with Mimi and Patrice. Nancy quickly dressed in black jeans and her blue sweater. She and George, also dressed in jeans, but a darker blue sweater, took the Métro to the Bastille stop. Once the site of beheadings, it was now a busy traffic circle with spokes of streets shooting out in six directions.

They walked several blocks to the arched entrance to Place des Vosges. A square of elegant townhouses made of coral brick and cream-colored stone surrounded a pretty tree-filled park. Nancy and George walked through the park and along the arcades at the front of the buildings. Nancy found where the photograph of the duel had been taken.

In one corner of the Place des Vosges, embellished by the blue-white-and-red striped flag of France, they spotted the home of author Victor Hugo. They walked past the little shop and up the stairs to his living quarters. Many of Hugo's original handwritten manuscripts were displayed under glass, although some had been lost or given away.

Once they were back in the bookstore on the main floor of the building, Nancy leafed through some of the photographs and literature that traced the history of the Place des Vosges. One photo identified the homes by owner name, including the one belonging to Juliette and Gilles Loiseau.

In one of the books, George found the same photo that Nancy had bought at the flea market. In the figure caption, Mimi's great-grandparents are named. The other man is identified only as "Antoine, last name unknown."

Nancy and George returned to the apartment for a late lunch of roast beef, cheese, and baguettes—laid out by Bess. "How did rehearsal go?" George asked.

"Pretty good," Bess reported. "I'm okay on just regular movements, but I'm still having trouble with the gypsy dance. I may have to switch off with Mimi at that point. I can hold Quasimodo while Esmerelda dances; he's just watching."

"Are Mimi and Patrice still rehearsing?"

"Just for about a half-hour more," Bess said, checking her watch. "Patrice is going to the library this afternoon. Mimi asked if we'd wait for her. She wants to go with us to Père-Lachaise."

By the time they finished lunch and cleaned up, it was after three o'clock. Mimi knocked on their door, umbrellas in hand. "It's starting to rain," she announced.

The Métro took them halfway to their destination. They had to transfer to a bus that let them off at the entrance to Père-Lachaise.

It began to rain a little harder, so they hurried to the gate. Once inside, they picked up a map and a listing of a hundred famous people buried in the cemetery: composers, artists, authors, and actors—even rock star Jim Morrison of The Doors.

The cemetery was built on tiers carved out of several hills. Each tomb looked like a miniature Gothic mansion. Weaving in and out of the lanes and paths, Nancy and the others climbed farther and farther up the hill to the site of the Loiseau crypt where Juliette was buried. As the rain pounded down, the paths became slick and slippery.

Finally they reached the top. When Nancy peered down at the tiers of crypts from the top of the hill, she could see what looked like a mountain town of elaborate stone houses.

Juliette's crypt was large, but not overly ornate. It looked like a small Greek temple, with columns at the front and a pointed roof.

As she stood there, Nancy heard a tapping noise. At first she thought it was the rain on her umbrella. But then she realized the tapping was coming from within the crypt.

As she tiptoed nearer, the suspicious sound was overpowered by a sudden snap of lightning, followed by a boom of thunder. By the time the noise died down, the tapping had stopped. Still, Nancy was sure of what she'd heard. She crept closer to the crypt.

One wall of the tomb featured a grimy stained glass window. Nancy noticed a jagged crack across a corner of the glass. The crack was wide enough at the end for Nancy to see through it with one eye.

Pulling her umbrella back so it wouldn't bump the wall, she leaned against the wet stone, and placed her eye against the tiny crack in the glass.

It was pitch-black inside the crypt. While Nancy strained her eye to adjust to the darkness, another sizzle of lightning lit the crypt's interior. Her pulse began to trip faster. She had only a quick glimpse, but there was definitely someone inside the crypt— someone *alive*. With another crackle of lightning, she saw the person walking closer to the window. Her pulse pounding, Nancy pulled back.

As the third flash lit up the cemetery, she leaned forward again and carefully peered inside. This time, another eye was looking right back at her.

12

The Clue in the Crypt

Nancy didn't move. She didn't breathe. She was frozen in the stare. Suddenly, the eye on the inside of the crypt disappeared. Nancy heard a creaking noise around the corner, followed by many splashes.

Cautiously, she stepped around the corner. The door to the crypt was open, and the sounds of someone running away in the rain dwindled.

"Who was that?" Bess cried, running over to Nancy. "Did you see who it was?"

"No," Nancy said. "It was too dark inside."

"Whoever it was is getting away," George said, looking through the trees. "Let's go!"

"We can't identify the person," Nancy pointed out. "It could be anyone out there; not necessarily the person who was just here." She looked at her watch.

"Besides, it's way past closing. If we're going to check out the crypt today, we'd better do it now. The guards are going to kick us out."

Nancy and the others took shelter inside the Loiseau crypt. The building was a cube about ten feet long, ten feet wide, and ten feet high. Nancy took her flashlight out of her backpack, switched it on, and moved the beam around the stone walls and floor. Chinks had been dug out of the walls, and little piles of stones were scattered around the floor.

"Remember the line from Juliette's journal," Nancy reminded the others. "She said the niche is in the corner that points to Notre-Dame—which should be that one." She tilted her head toward one corner of the room, then she turned to Mimi.

"Right," Mimi confirmed.

Nancy asked Bess to shine the flashlight beam in that direction. Mimi volunteered to watch outside in case the intruder returned. Nancy used the small screwdriver on her penknife to probe the corner until she found a crack with an almost imperceptible seal. Nancy and George chipped away at the crack until the seal finally gave way, revealing a deep niche.

Nancy reached in and pulled out a small hand-forged iron capsule. She twisted it apart, and pulled out a leather pen case containing a rolled-up piece of paper.

At that moment, lightning shot across the clouds

again and washed the cemetery with an electric glow. "There's someone out there," Mimi gasped, looking over her shoulder. Nancy and the others followed her gaze, but they didn't see anyone.

"That could have been a guard," Nancy pointed out, stashing the iron capsule with its contents in her backpack. "But we need to get out of here, either way." The others filed out, but Nancy lingered a minute. She took one last look around with the flashlight beam, kicking rubble out of the way as she backed out. Something glinted back at her from behind the door. She reached down and picked up a miniature golden tray.

She pocketed the tray with the capsule and rolled-up paper, and she followed the others down the hill. It was raining so hard that even the guards had taken shelter. Nancy slipped the bar across the front gate, and she and her friends left the cemetery unnoticed.

When they got home, William was waiting for them, standing beneath the theater marquee to keep dry. "I was just getting ready to write you a note," he said to Mimi. "Where have you all been in this foul weather?"

"Just touring around," Mimi said quickly. "We can't let a little rain stop us. Come on in—I'll make some tea."

Nancy, Bess, and George went up to the third-floor apartment to change into dry clothes. Then they joined Mimi and William in Mimi's kitchen.

"I understand you met with my partner this afternoon," William said to Nancy.

"I did. My father represents a group that—"

"Yes, Christophe told me about that," William said. "I'm surprised that you didn't mention it to me. I would have been happy to help."

"I told her that Christophe was a specialist in property law," Mimi explained. "I'm sure she spoke to him because of that." She poured tea and set out a basket of small ginger cakes.

"Have you told Christophe about Claude?" Mimi asked.

"That he is your cousin, yes," William said.

"Have you told him that Claude has a criminal record and has been bothering me?" Mimi said.

William fidgeted a little in his chair. He seemed to be nervous. "What have you heard?" he asked.

"Don't ask me how I know," Mimi replied, "but I understand that Christophe has met with Claude. Why would he be doing that?"

"I advised him to do this," William said. "I had already talked to Claude, and I thought it would be a good idea for someone else to speak to him too. It would help get the point across that we mean business. We were giving him the opportunity to stay away from you on his own, without having to call in the authorities to enforce it." He stood up and walked over to Mimi's chair.

"But we may need to go ahead and bring in the police," he said. "I don't trust Claude. I still think he had something to do with the arson, even if we have no concrete proof. And apparently he has an alibi— at least for the time up until the fire broke out. But I've always felt he was behind it."

"I agree that Claude is a prime suspect," Nancy said. "You know, we found that matchbox from Le Tricorne. Mimi tells me that you and your partner are members there. I understand it is a very elegant club. Not a place where Claude would be a member, I'd assume."

"No, indeed," William said. "At first I thought the matchbox might be mine, since I'm over here all the time. Or maybe even Christophe's—he's been backstage a few times. But we never carry the wooden boxes since the club gave us our gold ones."

"Do whatever you think you need to about Claude," Mimi said. "It's getting too dangerous around here to take chances." She told him about Nancy's experience in the bookstall.

"This is terrible," William said. "But I'm glad Nancy's all right. Mimi, you must be very careful. I don't want you wandering around alone until this is cleared up. Try to have a companion with you at all times."

William took a gulp of tea, then wiped his mouth with one of the linen napkins Mimi had laid out. "I talked to the police again about the fire. You know, Quentin is also a suspect."

"I assumed he would be," Nancy said, nodding. "It's because of the paycheck stub, right?" Nancy told him what Quentin had told them earlier about being backstage.

"That's what he told the police, eventually," William said. "But he lied about it at first. So he's still on their list."

William finished his tea in one more big gulp. "Well, I need to get home. Mimi, remember what I said. Keep someone with you all the time for a while." He kissed her cheeks, nodded to Nancy and her friends, and left.

After he was gone for a few minutes, Nancy got her backpack and took out the things she had pulled from the niche in the Loiscau crypt.

She placed the iron capsule, the leather pen case, and the scroll of paper on the table. Nancy decided to wait until later to show George and Bess the tiny gold tray that was still in her pocket.

Nancy handed the paper to Mimi. "You should be the first to read this," she said.

Mimi carefully unrolled the paper, scanned it, then spread it on the table. She held both ends of the sheet, so they wouldn't roll back together. "It's really hard to read, but it looks like a list of words—that's all."

Nancy, Bess, and George hunched over the table and looked at the paper while Mimi ran to get a magnifying glass. She quickly returned and held the glass over the paper. There were a dozen items listed. Nancy recognized some of them, and read aloud: "Notre-Dame, Esmeralda, Emmanuel, Quasimodo. Those are obviously characters from the book. What are these other words?" she asked.

"It's hard to read, but they look like other names," Mimi answered.

"There's something else familiar about this list, isn't there, George?" Nancy asked.

George took the magnifying glass and held it steady. "Hey," she said. "You're right, Nancy. It looks like the handwriting we saw in the museum this afternoon." She paused for a moment, then asked, "Could this list have been written by Victor Hugo?"

13

Quiet, Quasimodo!

"Do you suppose this is the treasure, Nancy?" Bess asked.

"Well, part of it, maybe," Nancy said. "If this was actually written by Hugo, that would be incredible. But I'm not sure this is the kind of treasure Juliette was hinting at. What do you think, Mimi?"

"Definitely not," Mimi said, slumping in her chair.

"This might be just a clue," Nancy offered. "Maybe we're supposed to use this list to track down the true treasure."

After Mimi left, Nancy showed Bess and George the small gold tray. Then she got one of the wooden matchboxes she had taken from Le Tricorne. The top of the wooden box snapped tightly onto the gold tray. It was a perfect fit.

"So you think this gold tray might be the bottom of one of those special matchboxes," George concluded. "The ones you read about, that the members of Le Tricorne get for achieving something special?"

"It sure looks like it," Nancy said.

"Like the ones William said he and Christophe have," Bess added, her voice a whisper.

"I'm not ready to accuse either one yet," Nancy said. "I need more facts before I show William this tray."

"I've got to get to bed," Bess said with a yawn. "This has been one long day. We've got the rooftop tour in the morning, and we go to the country tomorrow afternoon." With a tired smile and another yawn, she walked off to bed.

Nancy intended to read a little more of Juliette's journal in bed, but fell asleep before she even opened the book.

Friday morning Nancy, Bess, and George pulled on khakis and sweaters and reported for their tour of Paris Vu d'en Haut—Paris Seen from the Top. At three o'clock, they returned to Île Saint-Louis and met Mimi and Patrice backstage. Mimi had already sent a truck to deliver the portable theater to the Château de Berc.

"First, we pick our costumes," Mimi said. "There's a ball on Saturday night. Performers are encouraged to come in costume."

Mimi led the others over to several old trunks and a long clothes rack jammed with dress bags. She opened the trunks and pulled out dozens of costumes. "I think it'll be fun to dress up," she continued. "Besides, if we're in costume, we can get in some dancing after the show. I'm going as great-grandmother Juliette. This is one of her ball gowns." She held it in front of her and twirled.

"Very cool," Bess said. She unzipped a few of the dress bags on the rack. "Yes! This is definitely it." She pulled an elegant long dress with short, puffed sleeves out of a linen bag.

"That's a replica of Josephine's dress," Mimi told her. "She wore it when Napoleon crowned her empress."

George looked through a few costumes in the trunks, then shook her head. "I'm going as Louise Portier," she announced.

"Who's that?" Bess asked.

"She's a star French tennis player," George said. "So I'll just wear one of my own outfits."

"Not me," Patrice said. "I'm wearing something special. She pulled out a silver dress with a wide skirt and long ruffled sleeves. "This has to be Marie Antoinette."

"It is," Mimi said. "Your wig's in a box on the shelf. I'm going to wear one just like it."

"I found the perfect costume for Nancy," Bess

109

said, pulling some clothes from a linen bag. "Joan of Arc."

The others agreed it was just right for Nancy, so she nodded and the costume went into the pile. They packed up two vans with costumes, regular clothes, and personal items for Saturday and Sunday. Then they added the marionettes, sets, and props for their shows.

It was six thirty by the time they arrived at Château de Berc, which was about twenty miles outside of Paris. It was a gorgeous country estate, including a castlelike main house, many other buildings such as stables and guesthouses, and beautiful grounds with woods, lakes, and gardens.

When they arrived, one of the fair organizers directed them to a house in the servants' compound. It had a central sitting room, a small kitchen, two bathrooms, and six tiny bedrooms.

"I thought I saw you driving up," a familiar voice called out. Nancy and the others turned to see Quentin DuBos strolling toward their vans.

"You said you couldn't work here this weekend," Mimi said. "At least that's what you told me when I tried to hire you."

"Well, I was telling the truth," Quentin said. "I couldn't work for you because I'm already working for Pascal's. We are one of the caterers for the fair. We worked from three o'clock yesterday afternoon until one o'clock this morning getting ready." He smiled at Mimi. "I'm glad you're going to be performing this weekend," he said. "I'll try to catch at least one of the shows. Or maybe I'll see you all at the costume ball. Will you be there?" He looked at Nancy, Bess, and George.

"We sure will," Bess chimed in. "What are you wearing?" she said.

"Ahhhh, that's my secret," Quentin answered. "You'll have to discover that on your own." He smiled as he waved good-bye, then walked away.

After Nancy and the rest of the puppeteer troupe settled into their apartment, Mimi led them all to the rose garden. It was a charming area that filled the air with sweet and spicy aromas. Hundreds of trellises and arches had been constructed to hold climbing roses of every color.

The portable theater that they had brought was actually a collapsible metal building. It had been partially assembled by the people who had delivered it. The audience would sit in front of the theater on chairs or blankets on the lawn.

The theater contained the stage, the masked-off area above the stage where the puppeteers stood to manipulate the marionettes, and large areas on both sides of the stage. These two areas were like regular theater wings. Puppeteers could remain hidden from the audience in the wings when their marionettes were not needed onstage.

The wings also included locked closets where the puppets and sets could be stored safely overnight. Mimi and Patrice drove the two vans full of marionettes, sets, music, lights, and the rest of the equipment up to the theater.

"Ah, you made it," William said. He and Christophe were wearing dress pants, button-down shirts, and blazers. "How can we help?"

Mimi put them both right to work, rigging the lights and sound equipment up to the small portable generator.

"You're doing my favorite show this weekend, I hope," Christophe said.

"Yes, Christophe," Mimi answered. "You will see Quasimodo and his heroic exploits once again."

"It's nice to see you again, Miss Drew," Christophe said, turning to Nancy. "I have located some properties that your father's group might be interested in, as well as some excellent realtors. I don't have the list with me, but I'll get it to you after the fair."

Nancy thanked him and introduced Christophe to George and Bess. While the others talked, something flickered past the corner of her eye. She turned quickly and noticed that a curtain of roses twined around a white framework was jiggling.

Something is moving behind those roses, she thought. She strolled slowly away from the theater, skirting around the side of the long archway draped in yellow and pink roses. She took a few more steps and closed in behind someone in a gray costume kneeling behind the thick vine of blossoms.

Nancy ducked behind a trellis of white roses and waited. The person in gray stood and looked around. A gargoyle's mask hid all but the eyes. While Nancy watched, the sudden pop of fireworks in the distance seemed to startle the "gargoyle." The person hurried away.

Puzzled, Nancy returned to the theater and went back to work. William and Christophe helped a little longer, then had to leave. "We really need to work the crowd," William explained. "Our job is to get them to open their wallets this weekend and give generously."

After they'd left, Nancy told the others about the gargoyle she'd seen behind the roses.

"That's weird," George said. "It sounds like someone was hiding."

"Yes," Nancy agreed. "And I wonder about the costume. The entertainment doesn't start until tomorrow. It could be someone who's been rehearsing, I guess. . . . But that still doesn't explain the hiding."

Under Mimi's careful eye, the troupe laid the sets on the lawn and began assembling the ones for *Hunchback*. "This backdrop is awesome," Nancy said. "Was this leather work done by Jacques Guerin?"

"It was," Mimi answered. "Isn't it gorgeous?"

Bess, George, and Patrice stopped to look at the elaborate background scene. Carved and painted on a freestanding three-panel screen, the scene was familiar. A nineteenth-century Paris scene was painted across the three panels. Notre-Dame stood in the foreground.

"Wow—look at this!" Nancy said, pointing to a patch of green.

"Hey, I recognize that," George said. "It's Père-Lachaise cemetery."

"And here is Juliette's tomb," Nancy showed them. On a hill sat the stone crypt, with the word LOISEAU painted on the front. This must have been one of the special designs Juliette requested—the ones that she referred to in her journal."

Mimi asked Bess and George to help her finish unloading the second van while Nancy and Patrice locked the screen in one of the closets. When they put down the screen, Nancy noticed something odd about it. The panels didn't seem to be aligned correctly. "Hmmm," she said. "Something's weird here. We need to adjust one of the hinges or something."

They put down the screen. While Nancy tried to figure out why the screen panels didn't line up, Patrice started to unlock the door.

"Hey, this is already unlocked," Patrice said. "I thought Mimi said she'd locked it."

Nancy got a creepy feeling. She looked around, scanning the small crowd strolling through the gardens. Then she saw him. The gargoyle slipped behind another rose trellis, and this time it was carrying Mimi's Quasimodo marionette.

Nancy gently eased the leather screen into the closet, slammed the door, and locked it. Then she took off after the gargoyle, with Patrice close behind.

Nancy was sure the gargoyle hadn't seen her, so she and Patrice stayed a few yards behind him. They followed the thief into the château and to a doorway that opened to steep stone steps. They tiptoed down, grateful for the electric lights that had been inserted into the wall.

Slowly they descended into what Nancy figured was a small dungeon in a former century. Concerned that this might be a trap, Nancy proceeded slowly, following the sound of the gargoyle's feet slapping against the stone floor. She didn't dare even whisper to Patrice, because she was afraid the sound would echo through the dank, dark dungeon.

When the gargoyle's footsteps stopped, Nancy paused, motioning to Patrice to wait. When she still heard nothing, she stepped back into a small room at the side of the hall. Patrice followed her.

Nancy waited for a few moments, peering around the door. She saw a sudden glow down the hall— someone had turned on a light. She could hear rustling, shuffling noises coming from the end of the hall.

Nancy looked all around. Although the hallway had those small lights built into the wall, there were none in their little room. She could see nothing in the inky dark, and she wanted a better idea of where they were. She reached into her jeans pocket and took out her penlight—but when she tried to turn it on, nothing happened. She tapped it quietly against her palm, then tried again. Nothing.

Finally Patrice found a match and lit it. Nancy looked around to get her bearings. Then she nodded to Patrice, who blew out the match.

Nancy carefully stepped out of the little room and into the hallway. She was aware of every single movement of her feet, trying to keep her footsteps as quiet as possible. Pressing against one cold wall, she crept slowly down the hall. Her heart pounded so loudly in her ears that she could hardly hear the rustling sounds ahead.

14

Unmasked!

Nancy led Patrice slowly along the stone wall until they reached a corner. Keeping her face against the wall, Nancy could finally see around the corner to a small room with a large arched opening. Inside the room, by the light of a camping lantern, Claude Loiseau removed the gargoyle costume he had donned over his jeans and T-shirt.

Nancy ducked back, her heart pulsing loud and fast. Then she stole another look. Claude still didn't appear to know she was watching him. She didn't see any weapons, and considered confronting him. She decided to wait, though, and see what his next move would be.

Claude placed the puppet in the corner of the small room and heaped the costume over it. Then he turned off the lantern.

Pulling Patrice along, Nancy hurried back to the first small room and disappeared into the blackness. Claude's footsteps struck the hallway floor with a determined rhythm. He passed Patrice and Nancy quickly and walked on up the steps.

Nancy ran back to the room he had left. She grabbed the costume and Quasimodo, then led Patrice back out of the dungeon.

"There he is," Patrice said. Nancy spotted Claude strolling through the rose garden. She casually walked toward him. Nancy didn't want to scare him away. She wasn't worried about confronting him, because she didn't think he was armed. Still, she felt a need to be cautious.

Nancy draped the costume over her arm and sat Quasimodo on it. "*Bonjour,* Claude," she called out.

His head jerked around. The shock on his face quickly turned to anger when he saw what she was carrying. "Where did you get those?" he hissed.

"From the corner of the dungeon where you put them," she answered.

"You couldn't have," he muttered. For a moment, he looked very confused. He shook his head a few times. "You're just guessing that I was there," he concluded.

"No, I saw you," Nancy said.

"But . . . but you . . . ," Claude stammered for a few seconds. Then that iron-hard angry look returned to his face. "I don't believe you," he said. "You found those somewhere, and you're trying to pin this on me. It's my word against yours."

"And mine," Patrice said, stepping forward.

Claude looked from Nancy to Patrice, then back to Nancy. He seemed restless and ready to bolt. By this time, a small crowd of onlookers had gathered.

"All right, so what," he said. "Those puppets are Loiseau property. I'm a Loiseau. I have as much right to them as *she* does." He pointed to Mimi. She, Bess, and George walked toward them, followed by William, Christophe, and two uniformed guards.

"George came over a few minutes ago to check out the crowd," Bess mumbled to Nancy. "When she saw what was happening, she rushed back for help."

"Why did you take Quasimodo?" Nancy asked. "Why *this* puppet?" She wondered if Claude knew something Mimi didn't. Was this doll the key to the treasure?

"Because it's the lead character in her best show, that's why," Claude declared. "There's no reason why she should get all the property and all the business. And *especially* not all the treasure!"

"So Juliette's legacy is really what you're after?" Nancy asked. "All those offers to help Mimi run her business—you just wanted to get closer so you could find Mimi's inheritance before she did."

"I thought after last night, you'd stay out of my

hair." He flashed a nasty smile. "How'd you like your night with the books, little lady?"

"*You* locked me in the bookstall!" Nancy said.

"That's right," Claude confessed. "Broke the lock, threw you in, and jammed it closed with a piece of wood."

"And you set the fire in the theater and stole the other marionettes?" Nancy guessed. "And broke into the Loiseau crypt at Père-Lachaise?"

"I told the police and I'm telling you—I didn't set that fire!" Claude yelled. "And I don't know what you mean about those puppets or the crypt. I wouldn't need to break into it. I'm a Loiseau too, remember?" Just as he said this, the guards came and took him away.

"Congratulations, Nancy!" William said. "Mimi said you were a great new friend, and she was right! Claude's been the police department's prime suspect from the beginning. I'm sure the detectives will crack his lies and charge him with the fire and the thefts, too."

They all walked back to the theater. "We've been trying to get Claude to stay away from Mimi for months," Christophe said. "In just a few days, you managed to get him locked up. With his record, he'll probably be in jail for a long time. I say we all go to the Pascal's tent for dinner."

Mimi and the rest of the troupe secured the

theater. Then they walked through the rose garden to a large meadow. When they got to the Pascal's tent, Quentin was just ending his shift. Mimi and William filled him in on everything that had happened and invited him to join them for dinner.

Quentin brought out a luscious meal of duck crêpes with cherry sauce, *fleurs des courgettes farcies*—zucchini flowers stuffed with cheese and herbs—and raspberry sorbet. Bess, George, Mimi, Patrice, William, Christophe, and Quentin celebrated Claude's arrest and the end of the danger that had surrounded Mimi and her friends.

Nancy was there too, but not quite celebrating. Something just didn't add up.

Over breakfast on Saturday morning, Nancy talked privately to Bess and George. "I tossed and turned all night," she told them.

"Why?" George asked. "What's wrong?"

"I'm not convinced that Claude is the only culprit," Nancy said. "The police said he had an alibi right up until the time the fire broke out. The timing could be a little off, but still . . ."

"What if he had an accomplice?" George asked.

"Maybe," Nancy said. "Bess, think back to the night Esmeralda was stolen. Was Claude the thief? Does he match the size of that person?"

"No," Bess said, her eyes wide. "You're right,

Nancy. The thief was taller, I think, and not as heavy."

"And does Claude look like someone who can run across those rooftops?" Nancy asked them.

"Absolutely not," George said.

"Claude's description doesn't really fit the intruder in the crypt, either," Nancy pointed out. "Though I admit I didn't see that person very well."

"So Claude probably does have an accomplice," George said. "He doesn't seem to be the kind of guy who's going to keep quiet very long—especially if he can pin the whole mess on someone else."

"If the other person *is* his accomplice," Nancy said. "But suppose that's not the case. What if someone else is trying to sabotage Mimi's business or find the treasure? That person might feel more daring now. He or she might figure the police will nail Claude for everything and not look any further. That gives us a perfect chance to smoke out the other culprit," Nancy said.

"It's probably someone who knows Mimi, right?" George said.

"And who's already proved to be dangerous," Bess said, rubbing her shoulder.

"How about Quentin?" George asked. "He's about the same height as the so-called cat burglar. He's not as heavy, but the thief wore bulky sweats."

"Quentin has an alibi for all of Thursday night," Nancy reminded them. "He was working at Pascal's from three o'clock in the afternoon until one o'clock

Friday morning. So he couldn't have been the one lurking around the cemetery."

"Who could it be, then?" Bess asked.

"We've got two physical clues that haven't been matched to someone, and they seem to be connected," Nancy answered. She took out the wooden Le Tricorne matchbox left at the arson scene, and the small gold tray dropped in the crypt. "If that tray is the bottom of a matchbox given to a distinguished member of the club, then whose is it?"

"William and Christophe both qualify," George said, "and both could fit the physical description of the thief. And they know all about Mimi's possible inheritance."

"I thought of them," Nancy said, "but the more I get to know them, the more I believe that their affection for Mimi is not fake."

"But you *do* have an idea," George said. "I can tell."

"All last night," Nancy continued, "I couldn't shake the idea that I had a clue—but that I just didn't realize it. I thought back over everything that's happened in the last few days—even following and capturing Claude today. It was that part that helped me figure this out. As I remembered, a lightbulb turned on in my mind. Twice.

"Remember when I told you about how dark it was in the dungeon where Patrice and I hid out?" Nancy reminded them.

"And when you tried to use your penlight to get your bearings, you found that the battery was dead," George said, nodding. "That's got to be a first. You, without a working penlight?" She smirked at Nancy.

"But I did finally get a light, remember?" Nancy reminded them. "Patrice lit a match."

Bess looked at the matchbox. "Well, sure, but lots of people have matches," she said.

"Of course they do," Nancy said. "But check out the side of the box." She handed it to Bess.

"Paris is on the first line," Bess read. "Then London, Montreal, and Sydney on the second line."

"The last three are cities where a chapter of Le Tricorne is located," Nancy said.

"Aha! And Patrice is from Montreal," George said.

"But born here," Nancy added. "And she's a historian, so she has lots of resources available. She's researching a book on the history of Île Saint-Louis. Any information she turns up about Mimi's businesses will lead her back to Juliette. And there's something else: she's capable of skipping over rooftops with a puppet in one hand."

"Her gymnastics!" George said. "She was a collegiate champion, right? So she's got to be good."

"Exactly," Nancy said.

"But she's Mimi's friend," Bess protested.

"I know, it's hard to swallow," Nancy said. "But what does Mimi know about her, really? They haven't kept up with each other at all over the last twentysomething years. Patrice is a childhood acquaintance—just part of Mimi's gang."

Nancy cradled the gold tray in her palm. "Now, with no contact for over two decades—no letters, no phone calls, no e-mail—Patrice suddenly appears. Within a few minutes, she has worked her way into Mimi's business. She now has plenty of access to Mimi and her property."

Nancy laid the matchbox back on the table. "I'm not saying she's definitely guilty," she said. "I'm saying she's a suspect. She *could* be a member of the Montreal chapter of Le Tricorne. She *could* have a gold matchbox from the club. And she *could* have dropped part of it at the Loiseau crypt."

"So, what do we do?" George asked.

"We set a trap," Nancy said. "If she doesn't take the bait, we're back to square one. And we have to tread very gently and build a really strong case before we say anything to anyone. Mimi thinks this woman is a friend. We have to be very sure before we tell her otherwise."

"Agreed," Bess said. "Right, George?"

"Yup," George said.

"Hey, let's go," Mimi called to them, interrupting their conversation. She and Patrice stood at the door to Nancy's bedroom. "It's showtime!"

"We're on our way," Nancy called back. Then she

turned back to Bess and George. "We'll be coming back here to change into our costumes this evening," she whispered. "Let's meet then to set the trap."

The day was filled with music, folk dancing, country games and competitions, skits, food, a silent auction, and Mimi's puppet shows. After the final afternoon show, Nancy and the others locked the sets and marionettes in the theater closets. Then they returned to their guest quarters to get ready for the ball.

Nancy got into her costume and refreshed her makeup. When Bess and George arrived, she went right into action. "Okay, here's the plan," Nancy said. "I'm going to give Patrice a note to pass on to Mimi, and we'll hide out here and wait. If Mimi shows up, we'll scratch Patrice off the suspect list. If Patrice shows up, we'll confront her."

Nancy wrote the note:

> *Mimi,*
> *I think I've found the last clue. Meet me in my room at ten o'clock and the treasure is yours.*
> *—Nancy*

She folded it carefully, wrote MIMI on the outside, and tucked it into a hidden pocket in the sleeve of her Joan of Arc costume.

"Okay, let's go." She started out of the room, but Bess's voice quickly called her back.

"Nancy! Wait a minute," Bess exclaimed. "I just thought of something."

"What is it?" Nancy asked.

"Suppose Patrice *isn't* after the treasure?" Bess asked. "What if she's honest after all?"

"Then that's great, right?" George said. "No one's hurt."

"Except Mimi," Bess said. "If Patrice *does* give her the note, she'll come running back here thinking you've found the treasure. She'll be devastated when she finds out it was just a fake note."

"No, she won't," Nancy said, "because it's not a fake note. I *have* found it."

15

Merci, *Nancy*

The dance that night was held in an outdoor pavilion. Hundreds of costumed guests mingled and danced to a variety of music. It was a gorgeous night with a full moon hanging low in the sky.

Quentin, who had dressed as Napoleon, found his Josephine immediately. He and Bess shared several dances before breaking for refreshments. Christophe came as Louis Braille, creator of the Braille alphabet, and William came as King Charlemagne.

Nancy waited until 8:45 when Mimi was dancing to call Patrice over. "I'm going to get a bite to eat," she said. "Would you give Mimi this note for me when you have a chance?"

"I'd be happy to," Patrice said.

Nancy walked toward the buffet table, then side-stepped out onto the veranda. George slipped out shortly after Nancy. "Bess is having way too much fun," George said, "so I didn't remind her of our stakeout."

"No problem," Nancy said. "We can handle it." She and George hurried to the servants' quarters and Nancy's bedroom.

Nancy spread some important-looking papers and books out on her desk. They were props she had borrowed from the theater closet. Then she left the bedroom door unlocked and turned off the light. She and George hid behind the clothes rack in the corner of her room and waited.

And waited. Time seemed to crawl. Every time Nancy looked at her watch, only a few minutes had passed. She was sure it had been a half an hour.

"Looks like I might be wrong after all," she whispered. "If Patrice read the note and knew I was meeting with Mimi here at ten, I figured she'd get here way before then."

George looked at her watch. "It's 9:35, Patrice," she muttered. "Where are you?"

As if on cue, the bedroom door opened. Nancy held her breath. She could hear the rustle of the satin Marie Antoinette dress as Patrice glided across the room. She headed straight for the stacks of stuff on the desk.

With her back to Nancy and George, Patrice shuffled quickly through the papers and books. She paused and looked around the room. Then she turned on the desk light. Nancy gasped in spite of her caution.

"It's not Patrice," George whispered. "It's Mimi!"

Indeed, the young woman at the desk was wearing Juliette's antique ballgown. "Look again," Nancy answered. Telltale coppery red waves peeked out from under Juliette's wig.

Right at that moment, Nancy and George stepped out from behind the clothes rack. Patrice was so shocked that she dropped the large book she was holding.

"What are you doing here?" she asked.

"Well, it's my room for starters," Nancy said. "But first things first. Why are you wearing Mimi's costume? Where is she? What have you done with her?"

At first it looked as if Patrice was going to fight. She puffed herself up into a haughty pose. And then the air just seemed to whistle out of her. "She's all right," she said. "I didn't hurt her. She's locked in one of the theater closets."

"I'll go," George said, and she bolted out of the room.

"So, Joan of Arc, you are a fair warrior after all," Patrice said.

"The drama queen act won't fly here," Nancy told

her. "The smartest thing you can do is just answer some questions."

Bess burst into the room with Quentin. "Oh, Nancy, I'm sorry. I missed the time. But I'm here now. What can I do?"

"You can help me detain Patrice until Mimi arrives," Nancy said. Quentin stepped over to the door and stood solidly in front of it. Within minutes, George, Mimi—dressed in a robe from the theater closet—and William arrived.

Patrice slumped into a chair. "Okay, okay," she said. "No more games."

"How did you find out about the treasure?" Nancy asked her.

"When I was doing research for the book," Patrice confessed. "I'd already collected a lot of genealogy about my own family. When I began working on the book, I noticed a connection between our ancestors," she said to Mimi, "and to Victor Hugo."

"A connection," Nancy whispered, remembering the photograph she bought at Marché des Puces. "Did you have an ancestor named Antoine?" she guessed.

"You guessed it," Patrice said with a crooked smile. "It was my great-grandfather Antoine Gerard dueling with yours, Mimi—apparently, over Juliette. Antoine did not survive that day."

"I'm sorry, Patrice," Mimi said. "But you couldn't

131

have been plotting against me because of that! It happened so long ago."

"You're right," Patrice said. "What I was after was your treasure. I found some letters from your great-grandfather to mine. He talked about some important thing that would stay with the Loiseaus, and that the Gerards would own this thing over his dead body. This triggered memories of when we were kids. I remembered you talking about a family legacy from Juliette."

"So you figured it had something to do with the puppets," Nancy prompted.

"Of course," Patrice said. "If I were a puppeteer, where would *I* hide a treasure—or clues to one? I've been in Paris over two weeks, staying up in Montmartre. I kept a very low profile so you wouldn't know I was back in town."

"Honestly, Patrice," Mimi said. "It's been so long . . . I didn't even recognize you when you came up to us in the café. You didn't need to go to so much trouble to hide from me."

"Yes, I did," Patrice said. "I've been snooping around the museum and the theater for over a week."

"You set the fire," Nancy concluded.

"I was poking around in the storage room and had to light a match to see better," Patrice said, nodding. "The fire was an accident. Believe me, I wasn't interested in destroying all that material—or anything that could have helped me find the treasure."

"And you kidnapped the Joan of Arc and Napoleon marionettes?" Mimi asked.

"And Esmeralda," Patrice added. "But they yielded nothing. I was no closer to a discovery than I had been when I arrived in Paris. I decided it was time to let you know I was in town and rekindle our friendship. I figured if I was closer to you, I could get you to lead me to the treasure."

"Patrice," Mimi said, shaking her head slowly. "What a deceitful friend you've turned out to be."

"What made you look in the crypt at Père-Lachaise?" Nancy asked.

"I stole a book from the museum," Patrice began.

"My first edition about puppeteers," Mimi said, anger flashing in her eyes.

"I read what Juliette had said about being buried with clues and mysteries," Patrice continued, "and thought of her crypt. Unfortunately, you all had the same idea, so I didn't really have a chance. It didn't matter. I had no idea what to look for, or where. I chipped away at the interior, but didn't come across anything."

Nancy pulled the small gold tray from the secret pocket inside her costume sleeve and held it up. "When did you receive your honorary matchbox from Le Tricorne?" she asked.

Patrice seemed genuinely surprised to see part of her matchbox in Nancy's hand. "Where did you get that?"

"You dropped it in the crypt," Nancy answered.

Patrice shook her head and leaned back against the desk, a half-smile working through her angry frown.

"You didn't have the clue that Nancy got from Juliette's diary," Mimi said, quoting the line about the niche being in the corner pointing to Notre-Dame. "We found something in the crypt that same night: a list of character names from *The Hunchback of Notre-Dame* that we think is in Hugo's own handwriting."

"A list of names!" Patrice scoffed. "That can't be what Juliette was talking about. That's not worthy of all the references she seems to have made. Not nearly. Whatever the treasure is—if it exists—has to be something more than that."

A knock at the door announced the arrival of Christophe and a police officer. The detective requested that everyone in the room report to the station on Monday to make a statement. Then he took Patrice away.

"I'm sorry it turned out to be Patrice," Nancy said to Mimi. "It's not easy to find out you've been betrayed by a friend."

"Someone who betrayed me like that was never

my friend," Mimi said with a sad smile. "I'm just so grateful to you—and relieved that at last *all* the thieves involved with my theater seem to be off the street."

As Mimi and William prepared to secure the theater again, Bess and George gathered around Nancy. "Wait a minute, everyone," Bess said. "Nancy has something else to tell us."

"Even after I was convinced that Patrice was guilty, something occurred to me," Nancy said. "Patrice is right. A list in Victor Hugo's script is a nice find. But Juliette loved puzzles and cryptic messages. That simple list must *mean* something. What does the list refer to?"

"It's a list of characters in *The Hunchback of Notre-Dame*," Bess said matter-of-factly.

"Exactly." Nancy smiled, then continued her story. "If I were Juliette, I asked myself, what would such a list represent? George, remember the manuscripts we saw displayed in Hugo's home?"

"Yes," George answered. "Those were pretty cool."

"What did the text on the display cases say?" Nancy prodded.

"That many of the original manuscripts of all his books had been recovered—"

"But some had not because they had been lost or *given away*," Nancy finished. "That was it! The list of characters was a clue, a symbol, for the treasure—a full, original manuscript of *The Hunchback of Notre-Dame* handwritten by Victor Hugo."

"Wow! Are you sure?" Bess said.

"I'd been reading Juliette's thoughts for days. That's just the kind of puzzle she'd love."

"A full manuscript," George said. "He is one of my absolute favorite authors. That would be so exciting."

"And so valuable," William added.

"But where is it?" Mimi asked. "Where did she hide it?"

"She told us in her journal," Nancy said. "Remember? She said the leather artist Jacques Guerin followed the design and completed the puzzle for her. Come on, everyone."

Nancy led the group out into the rose garden and the theater. The full moon was high now, beaming a bright light onto the flowers. Mimi unlocked the closet door.

Nancy walked over to the closet. Gently, she brought out the leather screen with the picture of the Loiseau crypt, handcarved and painted by the artist.

"This is what I'd been trying to remember all day," she told the others. "Yesterday, when Patrice and I were carrying this, I had noticed that the panels didn't match up exactly. I was trying to fix it, but then Claude caught my attention when he stole Quasimodo."

Mimi stood next to Nancy. "I see what you're talking about," she said. "But I don't understand what it means."

"This screen is also different from the other ones in another way," Nancy said. "It's thicker—a lot thicker than the screens you use for other plays." She ran her hands down the leather panels. "I took out a few of these brads this afternoon. May I take out a few more?" she asked Mimi.

"Sure," Mimi said. "I'll help."

"We'll all help," George added.

Carefully Nancy pulled out a few of the heavy hand-wrought brass brads that attached the leather panels to the screen frame. She reached in and carefully pulled out the first few pages of a yellowed, but preserved and still intact, handwritten manuscript of *The Hunchback of Notre-Dame*—complete with sketches of the characters on the list she had found in Juliette's crypt.

"Oh, my! How will I ever thank you?" Mimi said, tears brimming onto her cheeks.

"A few gallons of ice cream from Café Sylvie would be a great start," Nancy said with a grin.

"An incredible discovery," William said in a breathless voice. "It's amazing. I'm in shock!"

"Not me," Bess said proudly. "I'm used to it. Leave it to Nancy to tie up all the loose strings!"